Watchman William

Ghost Detective

Watchman William - Ghost Detective

By Diana Shaw

Originally published in Great Britain
by Inside Pocket Publishing Limited in 2011

First published in the United States of America
by Inside Pocket Publishing in 2012

ISBN 978-1-9084581-5-5

Manufactured in the United States of America

www.insidepocket.co.uk

Watchman William

Ghost Detective

by
Diana Shaw

with illustrations by
Mike Phillips

INSIDE
POCKET

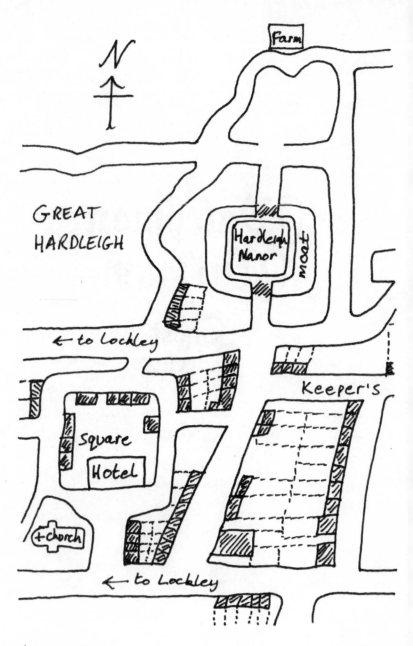

N

Farm

GREAT
HARDLEIGH

Hardleigh
Manor

moat

← to Lockley

Keeper's

Square

Hotel

+church

← to Lockley

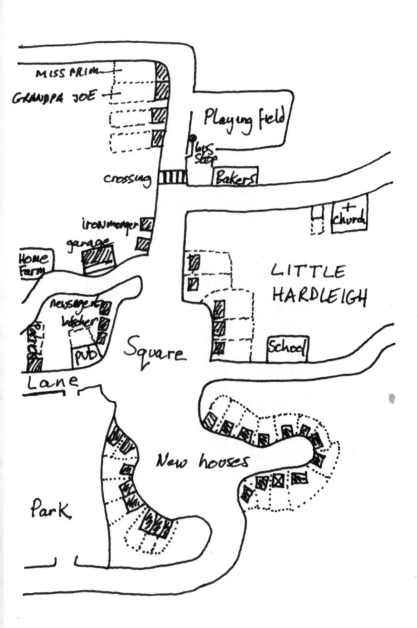

MISS PRIM
GRANDPA JOE
Playing field
bus stop
crossing
Bakers
ironmonger
church
garage
Home Farm
LITTLE HARDLEIGH
newsagent
butcher
Square
School
pub
Lane
New houses
Park

The Getaway Bike

'Here we go again!' grumbled William, peering out the attic window that overlooked the parking lot. He rubbed at the small panes of dusty glass with his sleeve.

'Hmm, even more families today; I know what that means. Noisy children everywhere dropping candy bar wrappers and putting sticky fingers over everything, and as for the grown-ups, well they're just as bad!' He looked around the little room. 'Thank goodness no one ever comes up here.'

It was his last stronghold at Hardleigh Manor. The villages of Great Hardleigh and Little Hardleigh nestled close by among the green fields and rolling hills of the countryside. For more than four hundred years this had been his home. Generations of the family who used to live here had always thought of him as their friend. Sadly, the last of the family had moved away some ten years ago, leaving the manor to the mercy of passing time and neglect. William had become very lonely and miserable as he watched the beautiful building slowly decay around him. He'd wished and wished the manor could be saved and now his wish had been granted, but not in a way he'd ever imagined! He remembered how it had happened...

...One morning, some months ago, he was enjoying his afternoon nap when the roar of a car engine shattered his dreams.

'Oh, fiddlesticks! Whatever's happening?' he cried, rushing to the window.

A sleek red Jaguar came skidding to a halt on the gravel path in front of the manor. Out stepped two men and a woman, slamming the car doors behind them.

'Camera, Max!' snapped the shorter man who was wearing a cream-colored suit.

'Yes, Boss.' Max delved into one of the baggy pockets in his leather jacket.

The boss, talking loudly, waved his arms and

pointed as Max snapped away and the woman scribbled notes on a pad. Her bright red finger nails were a blur as her pencil sped backwards and forwards.

Moving on, the men tramped across the bridge over the moat. The woman teetered along behind them in her pencil slim skirt and shiny black high-heeled shoes. The ducks wading below eyed these intruders suspiciously. Through the arch into the cobbled courtyard they went, where they were joined by an invisible William. 'I must find out what they're up to!' he told himself.

'Some of the timbers need replacing and the wattle and daub is in a poor state in places. As soon as the repairs are finished, we can give the whole place a few coats of paint,' said the boss. They walked through another arch to what

had once been a lovely garden, but was now an overgrown tangle of weeds and brambles.

'Garden's a mess; lots of work to do here. An Elizabethan knot garden is what's needed!' He strode off toward the house. The woman hurried along behind, scribbling as fast as her pencil would write.

'Knot garden,' she mumbled under her breath. 'Right...'

William followed them into the building. In and out the rooms, up and down the stairs they went.

'The visitor center will have a café and gift shop,' said the boss as the group stepped outside again. 'The parking lot will be round the side.'

After they left, William had sat for a long while on the little wooden chair in his attic trying to make sense of it all.

'It seems,' he mused, 'Hardleigh Manor is about to come back to life!'

Now, after weeks of comings and goings and hammering and banging, Hardleigh Manor was open to the public and poor old William was not enjoying it at all! During the restoration work someone had actually looked into his little room.

Luckily, they decided it was too small to be of any use, and so had left it well alone. At the foot of the stairs leading up to the attic, a barrier had been placed with a notice that read: 'PRIVATE – NO ENTRY', and that suited William fine.

'Time for breakfast,' he said to himself as he heard people moving about in the long gallery on the other side of his wall but reached by a stairway at the far end of the building. He closed his eyes and concentrated on becoming invisible before gliding off downstairs.

As William floated past, a short, stout woman stopped to button up her bright green cardigan.

'Can't you feel that draught?' Her chins wobbled as she shivered.

Her husband, who was a good foot taller and as thin as a beanpole, laughed. 'What do you expect from a building nearly five hundred years old? They didn't have central heating in those days you know!'

William headed for the café. At least these days he didn't have to go all the way to the village to find his breakfast. The buttery smell of warm croissants floated on the air and tickled his nostrils. He could hardly wait.

It might seem odd to living people that a ghost

should feel hungry but why not? After all, eating had been one of William's great pleasures in life. It was one thing he could continue to enjoy, so long as he always remembered to materialize to do it.

As Mildred Krupp, the rosy-cheeked café manager, bustled between the counter and the kitchen, a croissant left the basket and floated in mid-air to be quickly hidden beneath William's tunic. Mrs Krupp returned to serve an elderly visitor in a green parka who was tapping a coin impatiently on the counter.

'One croissant, please,' he said as she approached. Mrs Krupp looked at the basket with a frown.

'Are you sure you can manage another?' she

asked sharply.

'What do you mean *another*?' asked the man, his bushy eyebrows clashing together.

'Well, there were five in that basket one minute ago and now there are only four,' she looked around the otherwise empty café, 'and I can't see anyone else around here, can you?'

'How dare you accuse me? I wish to speak to the manager right away,' said the customer, banging his fist on the counter.

'Oh my, I'd better be off!' thought William, and he slunk away to his little hideaway in the attic. There was no need to open the door; he just passed straight through.

But when he got inside, he saw something that would have startled the life out of him, if he had one. As it was, he found himself trembling from head to toe.

'Oh!' he almost cried out in surprise. There, sitting on his chair, in his room, was a boy! A real, live, flesh and blood boy. William couldn't see his face very well, just a mop of fair hair flopping forwards. His head down, the boy appeared to be very absorbed in a book that rested on his lap. William hovered quietly in a corner wondering what to do. 'Nothing else for it, I'll have to scare him away,' he thought. Placing his croissant on the little shelf next to his jar of cookies, he gave his full attention to the problem.

'Hey, what's happening?' cried the boy as the chair began to shake. The book slipped from his lap as he grabbed the sides of the seat to steady himself.

'Oo-er!' he cried, as the chair rose up into the air until his head was almost touching the ceiling, where it hovered steadily for a short while. William could see the boy's face now, his bright blue eyes wide with surprise and fright, mingled with a tinge of excitement. The chair hadn't landed on the floor again when he leapt from it and ran from the room.

'Ha ha,' chuckled William, 'that'll teach him!' Materializing, he settled down to enjoy every delicious flake of his croissant in peace and quiet.

'Mmm, that was good!' he sighed, licking his fingers contentedly.

But then, he heard a

sound...

Crrreak! William jumped as the door opened a crack and a face peeped round. It was too late to vanish; the boy had seen him.

'Excuse me... I left a book in here,' he said, 'under that spooky chair. I wouldn't sit there if I were you!'

'There's nothing wrong with the chair,' said William, reaching down to pick up the book. He held it out. 'Here, take your book and off you go!'

The boy didn't move.

'Here,' said William shaking the book, 'take it!'

The boy still hesitated.

'Who are you?' he asked.

'None of your business,' said William rudely.

'Why are you wearing those funny clothes?'

'FUNNY CLOTHES?' William rose from his chair, placing the book on the seat. He smoothed down his tunic then tweaked his felt hat. 'I'll have you know I'm very proud of my uniform! People didn't find me funny when I walked the streets at night guarding them from thieves and vagabonds; they were grateful!'

'Sorry,' said the boy. 'I didn't mean to upset you.' He began to back toward the door.

'Just one minute, don't go!' It had suddenly

occurred to William if this boy told anyone about him, things could become very difficult for him. 'Perhaps I should explain...'

He sat down on his chair again, placing the boy's book on the floor. 'I'm William and I'm wearing these clothes because I was a night watchman at the time of Good Queen Bess.'

Thomas looked blank.

'You know? Elizabeth I, Elizabeth Tudor? Daughter of Henry VIII?' William paused, then added, 'I'm a ghost you see.'

'A ghost - wow! I've never met a ghost before!' cried Thomas with sudden excitement. 'How did you get to be a ghost?'

'I didn't choose to become one,' said William. 'It just happened. As a watchman I walked the streets of London every night with my staff and my lantern. My job was to watch out for anyone who was up to no good; villains, brigands, ne'er-do-wells, that kind of thing. I would ring my bell and call out the time every hour to let people know all was well.'

'Were you like a policeman?'

'Yes, I think that's what I'd be called these days. Anyway, all those cold nights – didn't do me any good. One day I caught the fever and, soon after, died. The next thing I knew I was a ghost! Well, I had my whole death before me and, not wishing to stay in the city, I came to the country looking for a bit of peace and quiet. I've been at Hardleigh Manor ever since. Mind you, gone are the days when I could wander freely through the house. This attic is the only room where I feel safe now. Didn't you see the 'no entry' sign?'

'I figured it was just to keep visitors out.'

'So you're not a visitor?'

'Not really. I'm Thomas. My grandpa Joe works here. He looks after the grounds. I'm staying with him and Gran at their house in Little Hardleigh.'

'I see...' William thought for a second. 'Well, you know about me now and I can't change that. But I beg you, please keep it to yourself.'

'I promise I won't tell anyone,' said Thomas. 'I'm good at keeping secrets.'

He reached for his book, then stopped, looking thoughtfully at the chair. 'Of course!' he said with a smile. 'It was you who made it move! How did you do it?'

'Telekinesis. It's a special trick of mine,' said William proudly. 'I can move anything I want just by thinking about it. Watch that jar on the shelf.'

Thomas watched as the jar left the shelf and

floated to the floor.

'Fantastic,' he said. 'That's a really cool trick!'

William gave a little bow. 'Comes in quite useful at times,' he said. The jar left the ground on its return journey then stopped in mid air. 'Can't resist one,' he said, removing the lid. 'How about you?'

As they munched on the cookies, Thomas looked around the little room.

'Who's that?' he asked, pointing to a tattered picture of a man wearing a deerstalker hat.

'You must have heard of the great detective, Sherlock Holmes?'

'Err, yes I think so.'

'The greatest detective of all times!' went on William. 'Imagine being able to solve crimes like him ...' He sighed wistfully. 'I found a book of his adventures in the library after the family left. The picture had come loose.'

There was quiet for a short time then Thomas looked at his watch and said, 'I really must go now.'

'I'll just check no one's around,' said William. He vanished and floated out onto the stairway.

'All's clear,' he said, opening the door. 'Remember your promise. Oh, and don't forget

your book; you were very brave to come back for it.'

Thomas picked up his book. 'Thanks. My mom'll snap if I lose it.'

William puzzled at the thought. 'Snap?' he said, stroking his beard. 'Why would she want to do that?'

'I'm always losing things.'

'I see…' William shrugged and reached for another cookie.

Secretly, he hoped he'd made a friend; he was tired of being lonely. He watched Thomas run off down the stairs. Back in his room, he materialized and crossed to the window that overlooked the courtyard where there appeared to be something of a commotion occurring.

'My goodness, what's going on down there? Who's that waving their arms? I must investigate.' He was halfway down the attic stairway before he remembered to vanish again.

As he glided out onto the courtyard he saw Thomas standing at the edge of the little crowd that had gathered.

19

'What's going on?' he whispered in his ear.

'Oh, William you made me jump.' Thomas moved a little way from the crowd. 'It's Patrick, the mailman. Someone has stolen his bicycle.'

'Left it here for just a minute while I delivered a package to the office,' the poor man was saying. 'When I came back it had gone, along with my sack of letters. I'll lose my job for this! Did anyone see the thief?'

'No, sorry,' voices muttered and people shook their heads.

'Someone swiped your bike, Mailman?' said a man wearing paint spattered overalls approaching across the courtyard. 'I was just through there painting a wall,' he pointed to an archway that led to the back of the manor. 'Someone came whizzing round the corner so fast my ladder wobbled and I almost fell off! A jar of paint was knocked over; made a right mess!'

'Did you see what he looked like?' asked Patrick.

'Didn't see his face; he was wearing a hat with the brim pulled down, but his clothes were very scruffy. I'd say he was a hobo.'

'The cash box has gone from my desk,' cried a young woman from the office doorway.

'Must have been the same person,' said Patrick scratching his head. 'Better phone for the police!'

'The thief will be well away by the time they get here,' William whispered. 'This sounds like a job for me. I know Sherlock wouldn't hang around; he'd be on to it straight away!'

'What are you going to do?' asked Thomas, but there was no reply. William had already glided off round the back of the building.

'Ah, a clue!' He followed the pattern of white marks left by the bicycle tires. After a short distance the paint had faded, but there was enough to tell him which path the thief had taken. Turning left, William set off down the lane that led away from the villages. At the bottom of the lane he came to a crossroads.

'Which way now?' he puzzled, looking straight on, then left, then right. He heard a siren and in the distance could see a police car approaching on the opposite road. 'Well, the thief can't have gone that way or the police would have seen him.'

The car came across the junction and continued on to Hardleigh Manor. William looked to the left. 'Now what's that I can see?' There was something lying in the road.

He glided along and discovered a discarded old jacket and... a battered hat with a brim. 'Ah, could it be our thief was wearing a disguise and he's getting rid of it?' He carried on round the next bend.

Ahead of him was a small car towing a trailer loaded with boxes and bags. One of the bags had tipped over and was gradually losing its contents onto the road. William swiftly caught up with the van as it came to a halt outside a house. He could see now the driver was Ruby Waddle from the charity shop in Great Hardleigh.

'Oh no, a false trail!' said William. 'I'd better get back to the crossroads.'

This time he took the lane to the right. He hadn't been going long when he found a bundle of letters lying on the grassy shoulder of the road. Quickly, he picked it up and tucked it inside his tunic. 'Another clue!' he cried. 'I must be on the

22

right track!'

Down the middle of the lane he flew, hoping
he might see the culprit at each bend he came to.
He was beginning to think he'd lost him when he
came to a farm gate standing half open. 'Bicycle
tracks!' he cried, looking down at the tire marks
in the soft earth by the entrance. He turned off the
lane and glided into the farm yard. There was no
one around, but sticking out the barn doorway was
the back wheel of a bicycle...

'Got you!' said William. It was gloomy inside
the barn but he could just make out a figure
leaning over a pile of hay in a corner. He was
definitely wearing a hat with a brim. 'I'll bet he's
hiding the cashbox!' William swooped forwards
causing such a draught hay flew into the air all
around the man's head.

'What's happening?' cried the man staggering
sideways. He tripped and there was a splash.
'Ughh!' He struggled to his feet and ran blindly
out into the farmyard, hotly pursued by William.

'Jim!' cried a voice. 'What happened to you?'

William stopped short as a woman appeared,
running from the farmhouse. Jim slowly removed
his hat as a ghastly looking liquid trickled down
his face. 'Yuk!' was all he said.

'But what happened?' repeated the woman, who appeared to be his wife.

'I don't know. One minute I was gathering up some hay when it blew up in my face and sent me staggering headfirst into a bucket of pig swill!'

William swiftly retreated. It could be a while before the poor farmer recovered from the shock. 'Another false trail,' he sighed, making a quick exit from the farmyard.

'Wherever has the thief got to?' He glided on round the next bend and came to a straight stretch of road.

'I can see something moving,' he said, peering into the distance. He picked up speed and as he drew nearer he could see it was another cyclist. Slower and slower went the bicycle up a steep hill. Faster and faster went William until he was gliding just overhead. It was definitely the mailman's bike, bright red with a basket in front for the mail bag.

'Third time lucky!' cried William as he swooped down and landed squarely in the basket, right in front of the thief.

'Pooh! What a dreadful pong.' He wrinkled his nose. 'The painter was right about the man being a tramp. The sooner I sort this out, the better! Time for a little thought control...'

The tramp was puffing and panting like an old steam engine as he forced the bicycle uphill. One last effort, then over the top and they were flying down the other side. It was time for William to take control.

'Ahh! No brakes!' screamed the tramp as he

tried to squeeze the brake levers for all he was worth. Then something seemed to push his feet and they slipped from the pedals. 'What's going on?' he cried, as the bike unexpectedly took a right turn. The pedals were spinning at such a rate now; another right turn and they were heading back toward Hardleigh Manor. The thief clung on to the handle bars, his knuckles as white as his face.

'Help! Help!' he screamed as the bicycle wobbled over a bump and swerved onto the drive leading to the manor.

Just as they reached the bridge, William slammed on the brakes.

'Blast off!' he yelled.

The tramp left the saddle and soared through the air like a giant bird, waving his arms and kicking his legs. *Splash!* He dove straight into the moat!

'Quack, quack! Strange bird!' The startled ducks scattered, flapping their wings in alarm.

Hearing the commotion, people came running through the archway just in time to see the tramp standing waist deep in the water, his hair festooned with slimy pond weed.

'He needed a good wash,' chuckled William to himself, 'but I doubt if he'll smell any better!'

Defeated, the man waded to the bank.

'Keep still, will you!' ordered the police officer who was trying in vain to snap the handcuffs onto the tramp's shaking wrists.

'That bike's bewitched!' the tramp wailed over and over as he was led away to a waiting van.

'Bewitched!' laughed the mailman. 'Rubbish! Imagine trying to steal a bike when you can't even ride one properly!' He looked inside the bag and took out the cash box. The girl from the office was so relieved. 'Thank goodness! Lucky we got it back before Mr Grimshaw found out...'

'Found out what, Mavis?' asked Mr Grimshaw, who had suddenly appeared behind her, rather like a ghost himself. 'And what's all this nonsense going on here?' Ernest Grimshaw, manager of Hardleigh Manor, was not a man to get on the wrong side of. Mavis quivered.

'It's all right, Mr Grimshaw,' she said, holding up the cash box. 'We've got it back now!'

Excitement over, Patrick the mailman picked up his bicycle and set off on his rounds. The visitors returned to their tour of the manor while Thomas stood under the archway leading to the gardens.

'William,' he whispered urgently, 'William, are you there?' But there was no reply. He waited, wondering what to do, when a ghostly hand tapped him on the shoulder.

'William, it's you!'

'Right first time!' laughed the ghost as he swiftly appeared.

'Where have you been?'

'Just remembered, I had some letters to mail.'

'Letters to mail?' Thomas was puzzled.

'I can see I'll have to fill you in on a few details,' laughed William.

He told Thomas all about tracking down the thief and how he'd controlled the bicycle and slammed on the brakes.

'So that's how he ended up in the moat! Oh it was so funny!'

Thomas and William laughed until tears rolled down their faces.

'Oh dear me!' William clutched his sides. 'I'll have to stop before I burst! You know, I've not had such a good time in ages.'

A voice called from the other side of the wall. 'Thomas, where are you? I need a sack for these trimmings.'

'Oh, that's Grandpa calling, I'd better go. See you later,' said Thomas and ran off. 'I'll come and visit.'

'You know where to find me,' said William, vanishing. Seconds later he reappeared in the safety of his attic room.

'Well, Sherlock, I wonder what you would have thought of my first case,' he said to the picture. 'I can't imagine you ever rode a bicycle!'

He reached for the cookie jar and sat down on his chair. 'How exciting, I've made a new friend

and caught a thief, all in one day! William the
Detective - I do like the sound of that!'

The Zucchini Mystery

William woke suddenly; surely, it *must* have been a dream! No, there it was again: a low rumble growing louder and louder, moving nearer and nearer. He covered his ears as the sound exploded into a thunderous clattering just the other side of the wall!

'Oh my goodness!' he cried. 'There's someone or some*thing* in the long gallery!' He closed his eyes and took a deep breath. 'If I just poke my head through,' he persuaded himself. Even invisible, he felt it would be safer if most of him remained on *his* side of the wall.

Moonlight streamed in through the small glass panes, the shadows of the leaded lights making patterns on the floor. As William peered down the long room, he could see someone moving. A

30

stooping figure lunged forward and the rumbling began again. He watched as a wooden ball rolled toward him, gathering speed along the sloping floorboards.

Crash! The ball hit its target and there was a loud clattering as nine-pins scattered in all directions just beneath him.

'Strike!' cried an excited voice. 'That's three in a row!' The figure jumped up and down in delight.

William's mouth dropped open in astonishment; were his eyes playing tricks on him? No, it was Mr Grimshaw: Ernest Grimshaw, manager of Hardleigh Manor, grim by name and grim by reputation. He'd only been at the manor for a few weeks but already he'd made himself unpopular. William had overheard Mavis, his secretary, chatting to Mrs Krupp in the café.

'He's so bossy and it seems I can't do a thing right. I've never seen him smile once; I think if he did, his face would crack!'

'Well,' chuckled William to himself, 'I wonder what she would say if she could see him now!'

The game continued until Mr Grimshaw gathered up the nine-pins and the ball and walked over to a shadowy corner.

'What *is* he doing?' William puzzled, as the manager knelt down and lifted one of the floorboards. 'Ah, a secret hiding place!'

He waited until Mr Grimshaw left then pulled his head back through the wall. Through the attic window he watched the lights go on in the manager's house. 'All clear, now for some fun!'

There was no need to be invisible as he glided through the wall into the long gallery. He set up the nine-pins and let the ball fly. *Crash!* Four nine-pins fell. He scooted up the gallery for another try. Seven that time, he was improving.

'This is a great game!' he said sending the ball rumbling off toward its target once more.

CRASH!

'Strike!' yelled William as all ten nine-pins fell.

Mr Grimshaw gave a loud snore and turned over in his bed, blissfully unaware the resident ghost of Hardleigh Manor was having such fun.

Just then, the first blackbird burst into song, perched in the branches of the tree beneath the attic window.

'Goodness! Dawn already, better get some rest.' William returned the nine-pins and ball to their hiding place and glided back through the wall.

Settling down on his chair, he yawned then closed his eyes.

'And now I know grumpy old Grimshaw's secret...' he said to himself as he drifted off to sleep.

***

William wakened suddenly to an urgent tapping on his door.

'Are you there?' whispered Thomas. The door opened very slowly.

'Come in, come in,' said William rubbing his eyes. 'I do believe I've overslept!'

'There's going to be a village fair,' said Thomas, 'with lots of stalls and games and competitions!'

'I went to a fair in Little Hardleigh last year,' said William. 'They had some stalls and a competition for who could grow the biggest carrots and that kind of thing.'

'Grandpa says the villages have taken it in turns over the years,' said Thomas, 'but this year it will be extra special; a joint summer fair in the grounds of Hardleigh Manor! He's very excited. He says his zucchinis are the best he's ever grown so he thinks he could win first prize!'

'Zucchinis?' William scratched his head. 'I'd rather have a nice, crunchy carrot.'

'The competition is to grow the biggest and best looking zucchini,' said Thomas. 'I don't think it matters what it tastes like.'

'I see...' said William. 'Anyway, when is the fair? Sounds like it could be fun.

'A week on Saturday,' Thomas said. 'There's a poster telling all about it by the ticket desk. I'd better go now; Grandpa needs help in the gardens. See you later.'

On the way back from the café, with his breakfast safely hidden under his tunic, William paused to read the brightly colored poster on the notice board. Suddenly, a door opened and Mr Grimshaw stormed up to the desk.

'This won't do!' he barked, jabbing at his watch. 'Three minutes late.' He stood tapping his foot impatiently as Mavis ran to let in the first visitors.

'And what is *that* thing on the wall?' He pointed at the poster.

'It's a-about the village fair,' said Mavis, turning the large key in the lock.

'Umph. Well like I said, I want nothing to do with it.' He turned and strode off back to his office.

'Grumpy old Grimshaw,' muttered William. 'Not a bit like he was last night. I don't understand it!'

Patrick the mailman arrived with a parcel.

'What's this I hear about a fair?' he asked. 'I hear there are competitions with money prizes!'

'If you grow the best vegetables you can win a hundred pounds!' Mavis told him. 'I've heard Joe the groundsman is in with a good chance.'

'A hundred pounds,' repeated Patrick as he walked away.

William scanned the poster. 'Ah: hoopla, donkey rides, fortune telling, coconut shy and ... now that looks interesting...' He chuckled to himself as he glided up the attic stairs. 'Could be just the thing...'

After breakfast, William decided to go for a leisurely glide around Little Hardleigh. He knew the house where Thomas was staying.

'I think I'll take a look at those prize zucchinis,' he said to himself. He floated round to the back yard. There was a small lawn bordered with beds of bright flowers and beyond that, the vegetable patch. The zucchini bed was just next to the rose bushes.

'My goodness!' William gazed down at the enormous specimens lying there. One in particular outshone the rest; it was no less than two feet long. 'I've never seen zucchinis like these before,' he said.

In a wheelbarrow nearby sat a smaller zucchini by itself. 'A reject, no doubt,' thought William, picking it up for a closer look. 'Can't see the appeal, myself. Ah well, I'm sure old Joe's bound to win a prize!'

William was floating back up the yard when he heard a voice coming from the other side of the hedge. He peeped over to see old Miss Prim. She was always neatly dressed with never so much as a single hair out of place. She even polished her rubber boots before gardening.

'Ah, Miss Prim,' people would say. 'Very prim and proper, just like her name.'

William was surprised to see her wandering up and down her yard chattering away to herself.

'My pretty pinks and my beautiful begonias, you have done so well; my radiant ruby-red roses, you're the best; I'm *really* proud of you!' She moved on to the vegetables. 'Magnificent mange touts! Superlative spinach! Perfect potatoes and the best broccoli ever! You are all just wonderful!'

'She's talking to her plants! I've heard some people do; it's supposed to make them grow well.' William glanced around. 'It certainly seems to be working for her!'

He floated up higher for a better view of the village. On the corner of Keepers Lane stood the Farmers Arms Bar & Grill. Mr Fletcher, the owner, was standing outside, chatting to Bob Smart, the newsstand, telling him all about his plan to open a restaurant in his back room.

'I'm a real chef,' boasted Mr Fletcher. 'And I'll be serving my own, homegrown produce!' Bob Smart looked doubtful. He'd never heard of Mr Fletcher doing much gardening; his rubber boots looked hardly worn.

'I've been planting cabbages, cauliflowers, carrots, cucumbers...' the landlord was saying.

'Broccoli?' asked Bob, adjusting his glasses.

'Of course,' cried Mr Fletcher. 'Broccoli, beans, bananas...'

'Bananas?' frowned Bob. 'Here? In Little Hardleigh?'

Mr Fletcher smiled. 'You wait and see,' he said with a wink. 'You'll be amazed!'

William's stomach rumbled. 'Time I was heading back to the manor for lunch,' he said. 'I wish I'd remembered to bring some cookies!'

Just then, Patrick the mailman came pedaling along on his bicycle. He was heading for home after finishing his round. William watched him turn down Keepers Lane.

'He sounded interested in the show. I wonder if he's growing anything he could enter? I think I'll take a look.'

About half a mile along Keepers Lane one ramshackle house stood alone, surrounded by a neglected yard overgrown with weeds. Patrick turned in at the gate and wheeled his bicycle round the back. He propped it up against a rickety shed and went into the house. William was shocked by the state of the vegetable patch. The runner beans had hardly the strength to run anywhere; they were sickly looking plants begging to be watered. As for the cabbages, they were little more than the size of sprouts.

His stomach gave another loud rumble. 'Definitely time for lunch!'

Back at the manor, William floated into the café rubbing his hands in great expectation of a satisfying snack.

'That's the chicken sandwiches done,' said Mrs Krupp, sweeping bread crumbs into a bin. 'Plenty there to be going on with.'

'Two won't be missed, I'm sure,' whispered William, helping himself behind her back. How wrong he was.

'Am I going potty,' said Mrs Krupp as she turned back and saw the gap in the line, 'or is someone after my sandwiches?'

Just then Mr. Grimshaw walked in.

'What's this Mrs Krupp, talking to yourself? Get a grip woman, you look as if you've seen a ghost! You'll scare the customers off.' He looked round the empty café. 'In fact it looks like you have already.' He helped himself to a sticky bun and strode off.

Mrs Krupp shivered. 'A ghost - now there's a thought...'

William glided off to his attic. He was glad to get back there for a while. It was tiring being invisible, and he needed to materialize to eat his sandwiches, otherwise the food would just float about in the air.

After lunch, he had his usual forty winks then popped a couple of cookies into his pocket and went off to see how Thomas was getting on.

Down in the ornamental gardens, Grandpa Joe had been trimming one of the topiary bushes; each had been formed into the shape of an animal or bird. Joe's stepladder was next to a peacock when William arrived but there was no sign of him. Thomas was sitting on a bench in a shady corner of the lawn, deeply absorbed in his book. A voice whispered in his ear, 'Not much gardening going on here!'

'Oh William, you made me jump! I was just up to an exciting bit. Grandpa had to nip home for a special tool.'

'I've been to see his prize zucchini - it's splendid! I don't think anyone else will match that!' He delved in his pocket and took out a couple of cookies. 'Cookie?' There was no one

else around so he could materialize to enjoy
his. They were happily munching away when
Joe appeared in the distance. Quickly, William
glided behind a tree to finish his cookies before
vanishing.

Joe looked worried. 'Thomas,' he said, 'there's
been someone prowling around in my yard.'

'Did you see them?' Thomas asked.

'No, just their footprints all around the edge of
my zucchini patch; one of the smaller zucchinis
has gone! I saw the mailman in the lane outside the
house. He said he was late today and had only just
finished his round. He hadn't seen anyone.'

'Mmm,' said William to himself, 'that is
strange.'

'I want you to go home and keep guard until I
finish here. Your gran won't be back from Lockley
for another hour.'

Thomas ran as fast as he could but William still
beat him to Grandpa Joe's yard gate.

'Now what is she up to?' he said to himself as
he came scooting round the corner of the house.

Balanced precariously on the very top of a
stepladder, Miss Prim was peeping over the hedge
into Joe's yard.

'Just as I thought,' she muttered as she climbed

down. 'I must do something!' She walked off up the yard and into the house.

Before William had time to think any more about it, Thomas came running up. Together, they carefully examined the footprints. All this time, William remained invisible. Although it was quiet in the village, he was worried Miss Prim might see him.

'Definitely rubber boots,' William concluded. 'Now this calls for some detective work. We need to measure the print and find out who takes the same size.' Thomas drew a line on a piece of paper exactly the same length as the footprint. 'Good,' said William, hiding it under his tunic. 'Tonight I'll take a look at a few pairs of rubber boots. Ah, here comes the bus from Lockley; I'd better be off now.'

'Can you wait a few minutes? I have a surprise for you,' said Thomas mysteriously. He ran off to greet his grandmother as she stepped off the bus. After a short time he returned carrying a paper bag. 'I figured a detective would need to make notes so I asked Gran to bring me this from the stationery store. It's a notebook.'

'How very kind!' said William. He took the bag and hid it under his tunic.

'Oh, I forgot, you'll need a pencil won't you?'

'No thank you. I have my quill pen and some ink in a pot. I just needed something to write on. I'll be off now; I can't wait to start my notes.'

Safe in his attic William materialized, eager to get to work. He opened his present from Thomas. It was a spiral bound notebook with a smart red cover.

'Wonderful!' he said, taking down his quill pen and inkpot from the shelf.

One thing was puzzling him: why would anyone want to steal a small zucchini? If a rival was hoping to beat Joe in the competition, surely the plan would be to get rid of the prize one? It was rather confusing, but someone was up to something and he was determined to solve the mystery. Now who had been behaving suspiciously lately? He opened the book and dipped his pen into the ink.

'I'll write the date on the top line,' he decided, pen poised.

Splat!

'Oops!' He moved down the page and began again.

Suspects:

Miss Prim - ladder - spying - said she would 'do something about it.'

Action - check rubber boots.

Mr Fletcher - talks about home grown produce but no one has seen his yard - rubber boots look almost unused.

Action - check yard and size of rubber boots.

Patrick the mailman - doesn't seem interested in gardening (probably doesn't have any rubber boots). What was he doing

*near Joe's house? Said he
had only just finished his
round - not true!*

*Action - keep an eye
on him!*

He put the notebook on the shelf and settled
down for a snooze; it was going to be a busy night.

The light was still on in Miss Prim's kitchen
when William arrived in her yard. There was no
sign of any rubber boots in the back porch.

Tramp, tramp, tramp! Someone was coming.
He peeped round the corner in time to see Miss
Prim leaving Joe's yard. She came up her path and
walked right past the invisible ghost on her way to

the shed.

'What's that she's carrying?' said William to himself. He floated closer for a better look. 'My goodness, it's a plant spray!' He sped round to Joe's yard. The house was in darkness; it was way past bedtime. What had Miss Prim been doing in Joe's yard in the middle of the night?

He floated past the roses to the zucchini bed. The prize zucchini was glistening in the moonlight. William bent down and touched it; the surface felt wet.

'Oh my, she must have sprayed it with something; it might die!' He quickly took out his pocket handkerchief and gently rubbed at the green and yellow skin. 'Let's hope that's worked. I'll come back in the morning and take a look.'

It wasn't until he arrived at the Farmers Arms he remembered Miss Prim's rubber boots. 'I'll check tomorrow,' he promised himself.

Behind the bar was a yard enclosed by a high wall. There was a wooden door that led into the yard. William glided through and what a surprise met his eyes; the yard was just a bed of soil, nothing at all was growing there.

'So what's all the talk about homegrown produce?' He made his way round to the front of the bar. There was the notice in the glass case by the door.

It read:

Opening Shortly
FLETCHER'S RESTAURANT
Sample menu:
Chef's special vegetable soup
Baked Stuffed Zucchini
Apple Pie and Custard
Meals are cooked to order using
our homegrown produce.

'Rubbish!' said William. 'How can that be? There's something fishy going on here.'

Mr Fletcher's rubber boots were in the front porch. He took out his paper and measured them. Spot on! They fitted the line perfectly.

'But they look as though they've hardly been worn,' William puzzled.

Deep in thought, he glided off to Patrick's house. After a fruitless search for rubber boots he returned to his attic and took his notebook off the shelf.

Miss Prim - sprayed
zucchinis with unknown

substance.

Action - Check zucchinis early tomorrow. Don't forget boots.

Mr Fletcher - Nothing growing in yard. Rubber boots correct size but hardly used! Home grown zucchini on menu!

Action - Keep a special eye on him - definitely up to something.

Patrick - No rubber boots.
Action - Still watch him.

William looked proudly at the page - not a blot anywhere. He closed his notebook, completely forgetting to let the ink dry.

It took him a while to get to sleep and when he did he tossed and turned as he dreamed of a giant zucchini chasing Miss Prim across her yard with a plant spray.

'Exterminate, exterminate!' the zucchini shouted. It had nearly caught up with her when William woke suddenly.

'It's no good, I must go straight away!' he said.

It was just coming light when he arrived in Joe's yard. He was relieved to see the prize zucchini was none the worse for the spraying. He went next door to measure Miss Prim's rubber boots; they were too small.

He was on his way back when he saw a car draw up outside the Farmers Arms. The door opened and out stepped Mr Fletcher. He looked furtively up and down the street before opening the boot and taking out a large sack. William followed as he carried the sack round to the yard. He was surprised to see Mr Fletcher put on his boots and fetch a trowel from his little shed. Now he knelt down and opened the sack.

'I don't believe it!' said William. Out came some fully grown carrots, complete with their green tops. Mr Fletcher picked them up one by one and planted them in a neat row. Next there came onions then four huge cabbages. The yard soon began to look like a real vegetable yard. He brought a wheelbarrow from the shed and in it he placed two zucchinis.

'The cheat!' exploded William.

The church clock struck seven and the villagers began to stir. Bob Smart collected the bundles of newspapers from the sidewalk, where the van driver had left them, and took them into the shop. Next door, the butcher was busy washing the floor before opening time.

As William came round the front of the bar, the first customer was coming to buy his newspaper. He parked his bicycle by a lamppost and tramped along the pavement, splashing through the little puddle outside the butcher's shop. His damp footprints left a trail to the newsstand's door.

'My goodness, it's Patrick and he's wearing rubber boots!'

As soon as the mailman had gone, William made sure there was no one near to see the piece of paper line up beside a footprint then disappear again.

'Well, we have another one that fits the bill!' he said. He looked down the street in time to see Patrick enter the hardware store. 'I'd better investigate,' he said quickly following.

'Wallpaper paste and paint,' the shopkeeper said. 'Doing a bit of home improvement, Patrick?'

'Something like that,' the mailman muttered as

he quickly left the shop.

'I'd better get back to the manor and update my notes,' said William.

***

'Oh my,' he looked at the smudged ink on the last page. 'I wonder if Sherlock had this trouble?'

Miss Prim - No damage to zucchinis; rubber boots too small; but what was she doing in Joe's yard?

Mr Fletcher - Cheating with vegetable patch. Rubber boots correct size.
Action - Continue to watch him!

Patrick - bought paint and wallpaper paste?? Doesn't seem to care what his house and yard look like!
Action - Keep watching

him; something's not right!

✱✱✱

It was Wednesday; just three days to go to
the show. Thomas had been on guard duty in
Joe's yard ever since the theft was discovered,
but had nothing unusual to report. It was a warm
day and he was sitting in the yard reading his
book. Gran was off on yet *another* shopping
spree. He shivered as a cool breeze suddenly
whipped up the dirt by his feet. The seat wobbled
a little as William landed beside him and quickly
materialized.

'Hello,' said Thomas. 'Are you sure no one will
see you?'

'It's alright. I've just seen Miss Prim in the
village. Now listen, I have something *very*
interesting to tell you!' He wriggled about on the
seat.

'Last night, I followed Patrick home. I've been
more curious about him since he bought wallpaper
paste and paint. His house is so neglected I can't
imagine him decorating. Anyway, the light was
on in his shed so I peeped through the window. At
first, I thought he was doing his exercises. He was

standing with his back
to me, his shoulders
rising and falling - up
down, up down. When
I went inside, I could
see he was blowing up
a large sausage shaped
balloon. Then he dipped
bits of newspaper into a

bucket of paste and stuck them all over the balloon
until it was completely covered. What do you think
of that?'

'Sounds like something we did at school,' said
Thomas. 'It's called papier-mâché; we used it to
make heads for puppets. When the paper dries, it
goes hard.'

'Well that *is* interesting,' said William. 'And
there's something else. In the corner of his shed
was a box of vegetables and guess what was on the
top…'

'A zucchini?' said Thomas.

'Correct.'

'Oh William, what do you think is going on?'

'I'm not sure yet. I need to update my notes and
have a good think. Don't worry; you just stay here
on guard.'

54

On his way home he passed Miss Prim. She was talking to Mrs Smart.

'May I borrow your recipe for zucchini soup, please?'

'Goodness!' said William.

Back in his attic, he reached for his notebook and read through his notes so far.

'Hmm….time to make some deductions.'

FACTS:

Miss Prim - used spray in Joe's yard. Rubber boots wrong size. Making zucchini soup!!

Mr Fletcher - Buying vegetables; passing them off as home grown. Zucchini on menu. Rubber boots right size.

Patrick - Making something strange in

shed. Rubber boots right size. Zucchini in box of vegetables.

'Well,' said William. 'WHO TOOK THE SMALL ZUCCHINI AND WHY??'

All through Thursday and Friday he turned over the facts in his mind until his poor head ached. On Friday night he paid one last visit to Patrick's shed. He had a theory and when he saw what Patrick was doing with green and yellow paint his fears were confirmed. Tomorrow was going to be a very exciting day; he must get plenty of rest and be ready for anything...

William woke to sunshine streaming in through the attic window. He smiled at the picture of Sherlock.

'Just the day for solving a mystery!' he declared. He looked out to see people already busy preparing for the grand opening. There was no time for breakfast; he glided down to the lawn beside the manor. Competitors were arranging their entries on the tables in the exhibits' tent.

There were the zucchinis, with Joe's right in the middle. There were tables for carrots and onions and some other vegetables. There was also a table for flowers. William floated round, reading the names on the cards. Just then, Miss Prim arrived carrying a bunch of beautiful ruby-red roses. She arranged them in a vase and placed them on the flower table with a neatly written card bearing her name.

'Well, well,' said William, smiling.

'I was worried about the greenfly,' Miss Prim was saying to Mrs Smart. 'My neighbor had them on his, but I sprayed them.'

William remembered Joe's rose bed was right next to the zucchinis.

The judging was to take place just before the opening ceremony at five minutes to eleven, and then the prizes would be awarded at three o'clock in the afternoon. People began to crowd into the tent; there was an air of excitement as the judges walked from table to table. They placed special gold, silver and bronze colored cards next to the winning entries. They were just approaching the zucchini table when there was a commotion at the entrance.

'Let him through,' shouted someone.

Patrick came puffing up to the table pushing a wheelbarrow. 'I sure hope I'm not too late,' he said, making a great show of lifting an enormous zucchini onto the table. The crowd gasped.

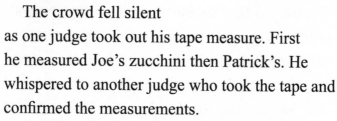

'Just in time,' said one of the judges.

The crowd fell silent as one judge took out his tape measure. First he measured Joe's zucchini then Patrick's. He whispered to another judge who took the tape and confirmed the measurements.

'First prize goes to Patrick!' Astonished mumbles filled the air. The card for the silver prize was placed next to Joe's zucchini. Excitement over, the crowd filed from the tent. Outside, the fair was declared open and the fun began.

William found Thomas standing by the entrance to the tent looking sad.

'Grandpa is so disappointed. No one knew the mailman was such a good gardener.'

'He isn't,' said William and it's not over yet.

Now you go and enjoy yourself and see what happens.' Before Thomas could ask questions, he sped away.

First stop was the deserted exhibits' tent. He lifted Patrick's zucchini and smiled. 'Just as I thought, it's as light as a feather.' William knew what he must do before the prize giving; it was time for his *secret weapon...*

Mr Grimshaw was sitting poring over some papers in his office when William glided in.

'Somehow, I have to get him outside.' Quietly William opened the window a little. Then he went over to the desk and began to blow gently across it. Several sheets of paper rose up and floated off through the window.

'Oh,' cried Mr Grimshaw, 'what's happening?' He ran outside and chased his papers across the lawn toward where the fair was taking place.

Crash, clatter, clatter! What was that?

Mr Grimshaw left his papers and began to walk toward the sound as if in a trance. His fingers were twitching; he just could not help himself. He stepped forward and handed over a bright fifty-pence piece. People nearby stood open-mouthed, nudging each other as Grumpy Grimshaw picked up the wooden ball and let fly.

'Strike!' shouted someone as ten nine-pins flew in all directions.

'Encore! Again, again!'

As Mr Grimshaw lunged forward for his second go, an invisible hand whipped away the central skittle and swiftly replaced it with the zucchini standing on end in a plant pot.

Crunch! Clatter!

'What happened?' shouted the stall holder; everyone pushed forward to see.

There, lying on the ground and surrounded by fallen nine-pins, were the remains of Patrick's zucchini.

'It's not a real zucchini at all,' said the stall holder. 'It's made of papier-mâché!'

✳✳✳

The last few stragglers were crossing the bridge as William and Thomas made their way up to the attic.

'What a day!' said William. 'So much excitement!'

'Grandpa was the winner after all; he is so pleased,' said Thomas. 'How did you work it all

out, William?'

'Well,' said William, 'the second I saw Miss Prim with the roses and heard her mention spraying the greenfly, I was sure she was not guilty of anything. As for Mr Fletcher, I knew he could have stolen the zucchini for his restaurant, but he will need a great deal more than one so it did not really make much sense. That brings us to Patrick. When you told me about papier-mâché, everything began to fall into place, especially as his jars contained green and yellow paint. I think he stole the zucchini to copy the markings carefully.'

'But what about Grumpy Grimshaw not being mad anymore? I'm not sure how all that happened.'

William told him all about the skittle games in the long gallery.

'I wanted people to see he isn't really grumpy; he just wasn't sure how to make friends. The idea of him hitting the zucchini with the ball just came to me at the last minute.'

'It was a brilliant idea! Everyone is happy now; Mr Grimshaw has even promised cakes for the staff every Friday!'

'So case solved,' said William. 'I think Patrick has learned his lesson. He was only interested in winning the money, but has said he is sorry. He realizes now a good gardener like your Grandpa gets pleasure from growing things. Winning the prize was just a bonus!'

'I'd better go now,' said Thomas. 'It's nearly dinner time.'

'And I could do with a snooze after all that excitement,' said William. He watched Thomas run over the bridge then turned to the picture of his hero.

'I hope you're proud of me Sherlock!' he said.

A Case of Mischief!

GREAT HARDLEIGH HOTEL - 'HARDLY' THE PLACE TO STAY!

'Now what's all that about?' thought William as he picked up a discarded copy of The Chronicle from a nearby bench. He had recently begun to take regular evening glides around the gardens, so as to enjoy the peace and quiet after the last visitors had left.

'I think I'll go and read in the shed,' he mused. 'Less chance of being disturbed. Grandpa Joe's gone home already.' Gliding through the double wooden doors, he found himself a comfy sack of compost by the window and sat down to read.

'If you are hoping for a pleasant break in comfortable surroundings, then the Great Hardleigh Hotel is hardly the place to stay these days!

'"I'm at my wit's end," Mr Hugo Crump, the manager, told our reporter. "It's been one problem after another, and now the guests are starting to complain. It's enough to put me out of business!"'

'Hmm,' said William, nibbling thoughtfully on a spare cookie he had found in his pocket. 'I wonder what kind of problems? I think I should investigate.'

He was glad of something to do. He was missing Thomas, who had gone home to see his parents and wouldn't be back for a whole week.

There was a photograph of Mr Crump in the paper.

'Goodness, he does look miserable! I'd better get down there without delay!' William said, brushing a few crumbs from his collar.

All seemed quiet as he glided invisibly across the nearly empty hotel car park. That was not a good sign; the hotel was usually buzzing with activity. He passed straight through the closed door into the foyer just as the lift doors slid open.

Mr Crump, the hotel manager, rose from his seat behind the reception desk as a red faced woman stepped out the lift and stormed across the foyer toward him. She was dressed in a bright blue bathrobe with a towel folded like a turban on top of her head.

'There is a mouse in my room!' she shrieked.

'Please madam, calm down; there must be some mistake!' Mr Crump glanced desperately toward the residents' lounge hoping none of his other guests had heard her.

'How dare you tell me to calm down; I tell *you* THERE IS A MOUSE IN MY ROOM!'

The door to the residents' lounge opened.

'Did I hear correctly? Did you say a m-m-mouse?'

'Major!' gasped Mr Crump as he stared at the trembling man.

'I can't possibly stay any longer; I'm off to pack!' The major took the stairs two at a time.

Mr Crump leapt from behind the desk and grabbed a broom from a closet. 'Show me this mouse!' he demanded.

William reached the landing as the woman stepped from the lift and led the manager to her room.

'*I'm* not going in!' she declared as she flung open the door and stood aside. William was first in the room. He definitely saw something small and grey scuttle across the floor and disappear under the bed. Mr Crump had seen it too; he charged forward and flung himself to the ground.

Backwards and forwards he wielded his broom, poking it as far under the bed as he could reach.

'I'll get you!' he cried desperately. He didn't see the little mouse as it fled to safety behind a curtain. William dove after it; he was sure he heard it squeak, but the mouse had completely disappeared.

'That's odd,' William said to himself, 'how could it vanish? There's something strange going on. I think I'll take a look around.' He went downstairs, leaving Mr Crump trying to console his guest, who insisted she would be leaving without delay.

***

'Pink sheets, PINK SHEETS! What have you done? How could you be so careless?'

William stopped to listen; someone sounded very upset. He glided into the utility room next to the kitchen.

'But it wasn't me,' protested a young woman wearing a red apron. She seemed close to tears as she stood before the formidable Mrs White, the housekeeper.

'It *must* have been you, Lucy,' boomed Mrs White. 'You are responsible for the laundry. Imagine putting a staff apron in with the white sheets; you'll have to pay for new ones out of your wages!' She turned and walked away.

'It wasn't me....' said the young woman to herself, 'but what can I do about it?'

'I must try to help,' thought William. 'Now, I wonder who else works here.'

That evening, back in his attic, William took down his quill pen and ink pot from the shelf. He opened his notebook and turned to a new page.

'Now let me see, what do I know so far?'

CASE: Problems at Great Hardleigh Hotel.

Staff:
Manager - Mr Crump,
Housekeeper - Mrs White,
Chef - Daniel D'Eclair

His mind wandered. 'Mmm - just imagine...
Delicious pastries dripping with chocolate sauce...
Oops!' It wasn't chocolate sauce but ink that
dripped onto the page leaving a black blob right in
the middle. 'Oh my!' He began again further down
the page.

Laundry/Chamber
maid - Lucy (surname?)

Other staff. - sous chef
and waitress - newly
taken on - names?

Problems:
mouse in room,
pink sheets.
Seems some guests
complained that they
woke to find windows

wide open in their rooms.
What next I wonder???

Clues: None yet,
but why is all this
happening?
Could it be sabotage?
Who might want to
put the hotel out of
business?

Suspects: No reason to
suspect anyone yet, but
don't know anything
about the new staff.

Action: Observe all staff
and guests and note any
suspicious behaviour.

William read through his notes once more then
closed the book.

'This is a tough one, Sherlock,' he said,

addressing the picture of the great detective. 'I wonder what you would do.' He considered the clues over and over in his head until he finally drifted off to sleep.

***

The next day he arrived at the hotel to find Mr Crump deep in conversation with Mrs White.

'Yes,' the manager was saying, 'you were right to tell the careless girl she must pay for the sheets. She's lucky not to have lost her job.'

'What happened about the mouse?' asked Mrs White.

'Well, there's no evidence of any more, so let's hope it was just a field mouse strayed inside the hotel. Regarding the windows, well it *was* a particularly windy night; maybe the guests in question hadn't closed them properly.'

'Let's hope that's an end to all the problems then,' said Mrs White.

'I sincerely hope so,' said Mr Crump. 'Now, about next week's bookings; that awful article in The Chronicle doesn't seem to have spread to the wider press, so hopefully any new guests won't have heard about the problems. Fortunately, not everyone has left and there are six more rooms booked for Monday; that will leave only two unoccupied. We must make sure everything runs smooth from now on!'

'Don't worry, Mr Crump; there will be no complaints about *my* housekeeping!' She smoothed her apron and strode purposefully across the foyer. As she opened a door, the tempting smell of warm baking wafted through. William followed his nose and entered the kitchen just as the sous chef removed a tray of fresh baked cookies from the oven.

'They look delicious,' said William reaching out. 'Ouch! Dear me, better wait 'til they've cooled a little.'

Daniel D'Eclair came into the kitchen carrying a book. He placed it on the workbench and turned to the sous chef.

'Usual Sunday dinner today Marco, but tomorrow we have new guests arriving. We will cook my famous chili beef! Here is the recipe; please read it carefully. I must find out from Mr Crump how many will be dining.'

Alone in the kitchen, Marco took out a notebook and pencil and began to copy the recipe as fast as he could. When he had finished, he stuffed the notebook into his pocket, just before Daniel returned to find him sitting at the table studying the recipe.

'That all looked rather suspicious,' thought William. He reached for a cookie and concealed it under his tunic for later. 'I must find out what else is going on around here.' He was halfway through the door when he heard Daniel say, 'I see you've been at the cookies already! Remember, guests first; we get the leftovers!'

'But I haven't!' protested Marco.

'When I was at school one dozen was twelve, not eleven,' Daniel said sarcastically. 'I must say, you did look rather guilty when I came back.'

Marco rose from his chair and drew himself up to his full height. He took a step toward Daniel. 'I told you...'

William didn't wait to hear any more. 'Oh my, I'd better go!' he said, gliding off to the dining room.

The waitress was clearing the tables after breakfast, under the watchful eye of Mrs White. Out in the foyer, Mr Crump was busy on the computer. William glided into the residents' lounge where he found guests sitting about reading magazines or chatting.

'Seems like a normal Sunday morning to me,' he said. 'I wonder how many guests are staying right now.'

Back in the foyer, he peeped over Mr Crump's shoulder at the printed sheet on the desk. Two names had been crossed out – Major Hitch and Miss Whimper (presumably the mouse woman). There were seven guests remaining, occupying three double rooms and a single. William remembered seeing three couples in the lounge, but where was the seventh guest? 'I'll take a look upstairs,' he thought.

There was a tray by the door of one of the rooms. William eyed the tempting leftovers from someone's breakfast.

'Mmm, strawberry jam!' A little plastic pot joined the cookie under his tunic. 'Now then, what's this notice? *Do not disturb...* Someone is having a lazy morning!' He paused to listen. 'But what's that dreadful noise?'

'The hills are alive with the sound of...'

'Screeching!' chipped in William. He chuckled.
'Sounds like someone trying to sing in the shower.
I'll wait until they come out.' Ten minutes later the
door opened and a tall thin man appeared dressed
for a walk in the country. William followed him
into the lift and took a ride to the ground floor.

'Morning Mr
Crump,' the man said
cheerily. 'I'm off for a
walk but I'll be back for
dinner this evening.'

'Oh, good morning
Mr Stride; I trust
you slept well. It's a
beautiful day for a walk.
Enjoy!'

Well, that accounts
for everyone, apart from
Lucy,' said William. 'There's no sign of her so
it must be her day off. I think I'll get back to the
manor and update my notes.'

Sous chef, Marco, William wrote, once
he was back in his room, *secretly copied*

75

down recipe for chili beef – why?

After lunch, William decided to pop back to the hotel to make sure everything was running smooth. All seemed normal as he entered the foyer. Mr Crump, smiling contentedly, was sitting at his desk enjoying a cup of coffee.

Suddenly, the peace was disturbed by an ominous rumbling sound overhead. *CRASH!*

'Aghhh!' screamed Mr Crump as he disappeared in a cloud of falling plaster accompanied by a deluge of water drenching him from head to foot.

Bits of wet plaster clung to his hair and eyebrows as he leapt from under the waterfall dancing about like an abominable snowman. People came running from all directions as the water continued to pour.

'Something leaking upstairs,' shouted one of the guests. 'I'll try to stop it!'

William followed him. Desperate, the man searched for the source of the problem until he came

to the single room.

'The shower!' he shouted to another guest who had come to help. It was a shower over a bath. The water, still pouring, had filled up the bath and overflowed. The first man turned off the shower and pulled out the bath plug allowing the water to drain away. The men went downstairs leaving William alone in the bathroom.

'That's odd,' he said. 'Who puts the plug in the bath when having a shower? Could this be another act of sabotage?' William was puzzled. He had heard Mr Stride singing in the shower but that was hours ago. If he had left the water running the catastrophe would have happened much earlier. No, someone must have done this deliberately, but whom? He decided to check on all the staff and guests to see if he could uncover some clues.

Down in reception, everywhere was a mess; a workman had to be sent for to repair the ceiling. Mr Crump had changed out of his wet clothes and was busy directing operations. Mrs White and the young waitress were mopping the floor. William checked the kitchen where he found Daniel and Marco busy preparing a mountain of vegetables for dinner.

'Must have been at it for ages,' thought William.

'So it can't have been either of them.'

He glided into the utility room just in time to see someone disappearing through the back door. It was Lucy. What was she doing sneaking around on her day off?

In the residents' lounge, three guests had just arrived back from an after lunch stroll.

'Whatever's been going on here?' a woman asked. The other guests couldn't wait to tell the story and all started talking at once.

Back in the foyer, William saw Mr Stride talking to Mr Crump.

'So we have had to move you to another room,' Mr Crump explained. Mr Stride seemed very surprised to hear the story. He certainly did not look guilty and William felt sure he had had nothing to do with the incident.

'I must get back to the manor now,' William decided. 'I don't think Mr Crump has seen an end to his problems. I'll consider the evidence so far and come back first thing in the morning.' He glided toward the door, passing Mrs White, who was on her way to the kitchen carrying a tray.

'Mmm, sausage rolls!' William turned to follow her. The sausage rolls were left over from the refreshments she had given the helpers that afternoon. As soon as Mrs White's back was turned, William helped himself to a couple.

'I'm sure these won't be missed,' he said. 'A detective can't work on an empty stomach!'

Back in his room, rounding off his snack with a smuggled muffin, smothered in lashings of cream and strawberry jam, he took down his notebook from the shelf.

'Now let me see....'

New Problem: Shower left on, causing flood. Sabotage?

Clue - the plug was in the plug hole! (Couldn't have been Mr Stride - too long after he left)

Suspects:

Lucy - sneaking about

on her day off.

Motive - Could be bearing a grudge about having to pay for the sheets! BUT the other problems happened BEFORE Lucy was told to pay for the sheets!
If this is sabotage she is probably not responsible.

Marco - busy peeling veg, BUT why'd he write down the recipe so secretively?

Action - Not much to go on yet. Still keep an eye on everyone!!

***

When William arrived at the hotel the next morning he found the staff all busy preparing for new guests.

'Four double rooms and two single,' Mrs White told Lucy as she handed her a pile of clean pillow cases.

'All *seems* well,' thought William. He decided to have a good look around the rest of the hotel to make sure. He followed Lucy into the lift. Before she had time to press the button, the doors slid across and the lift began to move.

'Oops!' cried Lucy as she struggled to keep her balance.

'Someone must have pressed the button up here,' thought William as the lift shuddered to a halt on the third floor. The door opened and Lucy stepped out onto the landing.

'That's funny,' she said out loud. 'There's no one here! Anyway, I wanted the second floor.' She stepped back inside.

'I'm going to find out who pressed the button!' declared William. He stood on the third floor landing and listened. 'What was that? I'm sure I can hear someone humming. I thought all the guests had gone out!' He began to search the six double bedrooms. In and out he floated. As he reached the third room, the humming grew louder.

'I'll just take a peek,' he said cautiously poking his head through the closed door. The room was deserted and there was not a sound; the humming had stopped.

'Mmm,' said William withdrawing his head, 'that was *very* mysterious.'

He finished checking the rooms on the third floor and moved downstairs to the second. Lucy was busy making up a bed in one of the rooms.

'What's that?' William heard her say. She bent down and pulled something from under the bed. '*Another* pair of shoes! I'd better put them with the rest.'

William followed her down to a little room behind reception.

'More for lost property?' asked Mr Crump as she passed.

'Yes, it's surprising what people leave behind!'

William could not believe how careless people were. Items of clothing were hanging on a rail. Shoes, bags and hats lined the shelves.

'Goodness, does nobody ever come back to claim them?' said William.

When Lucy left he heard a key turn in the door lock.

'Sounds like she's finished in here for a while; I think I'll materialize and go look around. Being invisible is very tiring!'

He looked at himself
in a mirror on the wall.
Removing his brown felt
hat, he picked up a bright
blue baseball cap and
plonked it on his head.
First he put the peak to
the front, then the side
then the back.

'Ha ha,' he chuckled, 'this is fun.' He kicked
off his shoes and tottered up and down the room
wearing a pair of ladies black strappy sandals.

'Oops! This takes practice!' he cried as he
wobbled into a clothes rail and knocked several
items to the floor. He bent down to gather them up.

'What a brilliant idea!' he said suddenly. 'If I
dressed up like one of the guests, I could mingle
with everyone and maybe uncover some more
clues!' William searched and searched but could
not find enough items to make up an outfit for a
man. On the rail was a bright green dress patterned
with red flowers.

'Oh no, I couldn't possibly,' he said, 'or could
I?' He thought about the great Sherlock Holmes.
'He was a master of disguise! I could be just like
him!' He was lucky enough to find a shiny black

handbag to match his shoes.

As he turned to go, he almost dropped it
in surprise. 'What's that?' he cried jumping
backwards. There, on a shelf just at eye level was
something brown and hairy. 'Ughh! Looks like a
dead rat!' He moved forward gingerly to take a
closer look. 'Well imagine someone leaving that
behind! It could be *very* useful.'

Gathering all his spoils together William stuffed
the lot inside a carrier bag he found lying about. It
was a bit of a struggle but if he undid the bottom
two buttons on his tunic he could just manage to
conceal the bag. 'Now for the rest of my plan,' he
said.

He took the bag back to his attic at the manor,
then glided down to the tool shed. As usual,
Grandpa Joe had left his jacket hanging on the nail
behind the door and sticking out his top pocket
was his cell phone. William took out a bit of paper
with the number on. He pressed the keys carefully
and held the phone to his ear. Nothing happened.
He looked at the keyboard and spotted a little
green phone symbol.

'I wonder...' he thought, and pressed it. After
a couple of rings, a voice answered. 'Great
Hardleigh Hotel, may I help?'

'Indeed you may,' said William in a high pitched voice. 'I would like to book a room please...'

✱✱✱

'Eighteen for dinner, we've just had a last minute booking,' Mr Crump said to Daniel. 'And Lucy, you'll need to make up the bed in room nine please. We're expecting a Miss err... (he glanced at the pad by the telephone) Tudor.'

Right on cue, William made his grand entrance. Everyone stopped to stare as he walked slowly across the foyer. The dress fitted well and he'd just about mastered the art of walking in high heels. But the crowning glory was his beautiful shoulder length auburn hair.

After checking in, he was directed to his room on the first floor. He opened the small suitcase he had 'borrowed' from Mr Grimshaw's attic and unpacked his watchman's clothes.

Dong, dong, dong! Downstairs, the gong

85

was calling the guests to dinner. Quick, William hung up his clothes in the wardrobe and went down to the restaurant. He was enjoying being undercover, Sherlock was not the only master of disguise.

'Something rather odd happened last night,' a man on the next table was saying. 'I couldn't sleep, so I switched on the light and reached for my book but it wasn't there!'

'Not there?' asked a woman. 'You mean it had disappeared?'

'Not exactly,' said the man. 'It had moved. Strangest thing, I found it in the bathroom!'

'Now you come to mention it,' said another guest, 'I couldn't figure out how one of my slippers had found its way out onto the landing!'

Before anyone could comment, Daniel strode into the room. 'Good evening ladies and gentlemen. Tonight I will delight you all with my famous chili beef. Enjoy!'

There was loud applause as the waitress started serving the meal.

'I'm looking forward to this,' said a woman picking up her knife and fork.

There was a hush as everyone took the first eagerly anticipated mouthful.

86

William was just about to open *his* mouth when...

'Ahh!' screamed someone. 'Help, I'm on fire!'

'Water! Water!'

Chairs toppled over as people jumped up from their seats wafting their hands in front of their mouths. Mr Crump and Mrs White rushed to the rescue with jugs of iced water.

Amidst all the fuss, William leapt into action. Invisible, he made his way to the kitchen.

'Incompetent fool! Call yourself a chef!' Daniel's face was bright red as he confronted his sous chef.

'But I swear I only put in the right amount of chili powder!' cried Marco.

'There's one way to prove it. Where's the jar?'

Marco looked on the shelf where the herbs and spices were kept.

'I put it right there,' he said pointing to a space, 'but it's gone!'

'Don't be ridiculous,' said Daniel.

Something fell from Marco's pocket as Daniel pushed past him to look.

'What's that?' demanded Daniel as Marco tried to conceal his notebook.

'I wonder how he'll explain that one?' said

William.

'Daniel!' roared Mr Crump from the restaurant. 'More iced water!'

Daniel and Marco both jumped, fumbling for the tap and a water jug at the same time. The explanation would have to wait.

Returning to his room, William changed back into his own clothes, listing all the problems in his mind as he did so.

Mouse!

Open windows!

Pink sheets!

Flooded Bath!

Chili poisoning!

The more he thought, the more they all seemed like attempts to put the hotel out of business. But what happened to the mouse? And who else but Lucy had the opportunity to put the apron in with the sheets?

If someone *had* opened the windows, they would have had to go into guests' rooms in the middle of the night: very risky! How could the shower have been switched on if everyone was downstairs or away from the hotel? And what had happened to the chili powder?

Then there were complaints from the guests

their belongings had been moved and the mysterious humming he had heard. Poor William, his head was aching as he tried to think.

'Hee hee hee!' Someone was chuckling nearby.

William glided out onto the landing; there was no one around.

'Hee hee!' There it was again.

'It's coming from round that corner,' said William, speeding along the landing, gradually becoming invisible as he went.

As he turned the corner something floated through the air. It was a small hammer and it was heading for the glass case that housed the fire alarm; William grabbed the hammer and found himself struggling against an invisible force. He pulled and pulled until the hammer was his.

'Stop!' he shouted as a cool blast of air breezed past him. 'The game's up; stop and show yourself!' He followed the breeze, waving the hammer wildly.

'Ouch!' cried a voice. 'Alright, I give up.'

William materialized quick; they had stopped right outside his room.

'Come in here,' he ordered.

He watched as the other ghost slowly appeared. A shock of bright orange hair crowned his

head. His face was painted white and his bulbous
nose a brilliant red. There were circles of red
on his cheeks too and his painted red lips were
surrounded by an oval of vivid yellow.

'A clown!' cried William, as the ghost's baggy,
multi-colored costume and long pointed shoes
appeared.

The clown stared at William as he rubbed the
bump on his head. 'That hurt!' he said.

'Not as much as the hurt you've been causing
around here,' said William. 'You've caused no end
of problems for poor Mr Crump; you've almost
put him out of business! As for that latest bit of
tomfoolery, I suppose you would have found

it very funny if all the guests had had to stand outside on a cold dark night; not to mention the fire department being called on for nothing!'

The clown glared defiantly at William. 'I was just having a bit of fun,' he said.

'A bit of fun!?' exploded William. 'How dare you? You're a disgrace to... to Ghosthood! Who do you think you were?'

The clown ruffled his hair.

'My name is Binky; I was a clown in Victorian England. I love getting up to mischief. I can't help it; it's in my nature. This is the best place I've ever stayed!'

'Well you can't stay any longer; you must leave at once!'

'Make me!' said the clown. He placed the tip of his thumb on his nose and wiggled his fingers rudely.

'I certainly will,' shouted William. 'Watch this!' In seconds, he became Miss Tudor once more.

The clown roared with laughter. 'You look ridiculous!' he said.

'You won't think me ridiculous when I complain to the manager about the ghost in my room. He'll send for the Spook Squad straight away to get you busted!' William walked toward the door.

'Spook Squad! Oh no! Please, not them!'

William turned to face Binky who was shivering from head to toe.

'Well?' he asked.

'Alright, you win,' groaned Binky. 'But where can I go?'

William thought for a short time. 'I know just the place,' he said. 'The traveling fair is visiting Lockley for a short time. I think working on the ghost train would be just the thing for you!'

'Roll up! Roll up! All aboard for a spooky ride!'

Thomas handed over his pound and found an empty car.

'William, are you there?' he whispered as the train suddenly set off toward the forbidding black doors.

'Yes,' chuckled William seated invisibly opposite his young friend. 'Prepare to have some fun!'

The doors creaked open and the train disappeared into the darkness as the passengers shrieked and screamed in nervous excitement.

'Ugh!' cried Thomas raising his arm as

something furry brushed across his face. A light flashed on and off and for just that short time he saw a gigantic web where a monstrous orange and black spider waved his legs menacingly. 'Help!' Thomas shouted.

'Great isn't it?' laughed William.

'Oooh! Oooh!' A spine chilling moaning filled the air then a clanking sound, as an eerie light illuminated a hooded figure dragging a ball and chain.

There were screams as the figure came toward the train. Nearer and nearer came the apparition, louder and louder grew the moaning. Long, spindly arms reached out toward them...

'Ahh!' cried Thomas covering his head. Nothing happened. When he dared to peep, the ghost had vanished.

'Just round this next bend!' William shouted as the train rattled on.

Music was playing: strange tinkling music like the sound of an old hurdy gurdy. The train came to a sudden halt. Thomas could hear the trembling voices of the other passengers.

'What's happening? Why have we stopped?'

He peered into the darkness. 'W-William,' he whispered.

Bang! Flash! With the clash of a cymbal the tunnel was flooded with light.

'Here he comes!' shouted William and out from nowhere stepped the colorful figure of Binky, the clown.

Binky performed the most amazing somersaults in mid air then lay down a few feet off the ground with nothing apparently visible to support him. Next, he stood with his arms folded while he juggled several balls in the air just by looking at them.

'Whoooo!' he glided toward the train, swooping over the heads of the shrieking passengers as he swirled round and round and round. As his ghostly circus act came to an end, he entertained his audience by disappearing a little at a time until only his painted face and bright orange hair remained hovering in the fading light. Then, with a grin and a ghostly giggle, he vanished.

The light went out and the train rumbled on until it reached the doors and burst out into the daylight.

Thomas rubbed his eyes. 'That was great, William!' he said. 'I'm sorry I missed all the fun at the hotel, but I'm glad I came back in time to see Binky before the fair moves on.' He climbed from the car as William whispered, 'Meet me behind that caravan near those trees; it should be quiet enough to materialize.'

By the time Thomas reached the caravan William was there waiting, holding a huge pink cotton candy in each hand.

'Cool! How did you manage that?'

William just smiled.

'So that's what happened to Binky, but you didn't tell me what Marco the sous chef was up to.'

'Well,' said William, licking his sticky fingers, 'it turned out he's planning to open his own restaurant in Lockley and wanted to steal Daniel's famous recipe. He's very sorry; in fact they are friends now and Daniel has offered to help him out with some ideas.'

'So everything is all right now?'

'Yes. Though Mr Crump has no idea who caused all the problems. He's just happy the hotel is running good and smooth again. He even gave Lucy her wages back!'

'I wish I'd seen you dressed as Miss Tudor.'

'I don't think that will be happening again!' laughed William.

'Well, I'm not going to miss any more adventures,' said Thomas. 'Dad will be working abroad until Christmas and Mom is going with him. I'll be staying with Gran and Grandpa for a while, so I can see you every day!'

'That's great news!' said William. 'I'm sure we'll have some more crimes to solve before long!'

'Let's hope we don't run into any more ghosts though, hey?' said Thomas. 'You never know what to expect.'

'I quite agree,' said William with a smile. 'Very unpredictable!'

The Case of the
Missing Money

'Good luck,' whispered William.

'Don't worry,' said Thomas. 'I've made a few friends in the village already; I won't be lonely! See you later.'

William raised an invisible hand as Thomas ran across the playground to join some boys searching for horse chestnuts beneath an old chestnut tree.

'First day of term already, I can't believe the vacation is over,' said one woman to another standing nearby.

Clang! Clang! Clang!

At the sound of the bell, the children quickly joined their lines and filed into the building.

'I wonder what school's like?' thought William as he glided back down the village high street. As a child from a poor family he never went to school. He'd learned to read a little and to copy some words by watching and listening to others when he was out and about. Since becoming a ghost he had taught himself a great deal more. In the early days, when the family lived at the manor, he'd spent hours in the library studying the books.

He joined the visitors, queuing for refreshments in the manor café. It was so busy no one noticed when two iced buns and a bottle of lemonade floated off the counter and out of sight under his tunic. Back in the attic he placed his spoils on the shelf, then popped a couple of cookies into his pocket and went off for a stroll round the gardens. In the orchard were picnic tables and on such a lovely day people were gathering to eat their lunch outside.

William found an empty bench and sat watching the ducks on the moat, squabbling over scraps thrown to them. The woman on the next bench was enjoying an ice cream while chatting to her friend.

'Heh! What's that?'

William looked over to see her having a tug of war with a little duck that had snuck under her seat

and was pulling at the end of her ice cream cone.

Snap! The duck waddled off and glided onto the moat, swallowing the piece of cookie in one gulp.

'The cheek of it,' said the woman but she couldn't help laughing.

'There's work to be done before Thomas arrives!' William said to himself and glided off up to his room.

Once there, he set a small wooden table with two plastic cups and a bottle of lemonade. He then placed the two buns from the café on paper napkins. Next he tidied his shelf, making sure his notebook full of clues and ink pot and quill stood neatly arranged. On the wall, the picture of

Sherlock looked down on him; he noticed the great detective leaned a little to one side.

'That won't do!' William carefully straightened the picture, then took down his copy of the great man's adventures and settled down into his comfy chair.

'Now, where was I up to? Ah, yes! "The Carbuncle!"'

At half past three, he closed his book and stood watching by the window.

'There he is!' he cried at last, seeing Thomas running over the bridge toward the manor.

'I thought you were never coming,' said William as the young lad burst into the room.

'I had to go home first to change out of my sports kit and to collect something for you.'

'For me?'

He reached into his pocket then handed William a cellphone.

'It's my old one,' Thomas said. 'It still works. I've charged up the battery and there's about five pounds credit left on it. I figured it would be useful if we need to get in touch urgently when we are doing detective work. I've put in my number for you. Try it. Just press *phone book* then *Thomas*.'

William tried.

Meow! Meow! Meow!

Thomas laughed and took out his cellphone.

'Do you like the ringtone?' he asked. 'Look, I press this to answer the call. Now I'll call you.'

William almost dropped his cellphone when it began to bark.

Woof! Woof! Woof!

'This is real good,' he said when he stopped laughing. 'We can get in touch whenever we need to!'

'Switch it off for now to save the battery,' said Thomas.

William carefully placed the cellphone on his shelf and turned to Thomas.

'Well, what was school like?' he asked eagerly.

'Brilliant!' said Thomas between mouthfuls of sticky iced bun. He took a drink of lemonade. 'I'm going to be on the soccer team!'

'That's great! And what else happened today?'

'Besides games, we had math and singing and we started our history project. You won't believe it; it's all about Tudor times!'

'How about that,' said William. 'I may be able to help out with your homework.'

'Mrs Ward was going to get a pedlar from Tudor times to tell us all about his life but he can't come.'

'What do you mean?' asked William. 'Is there another ghost around?'

'Not a ghost,' laughed Thomas. 'It would be an actor dressed up.'

'Hmm, what could *he* tell you?' He stroked his chin thoughtfully. 'Now, if I come...'

'You!'

'Why not?' William began to glide up and down the room in excitement. 'I'd be perfect!' he said.

Before Thomas could say another word, he took down his lantern, and then from a closet in

the corner he produced a long wooden staff and a hand bell.

He rang the bell and called out, 'Twelve of the clock, look well to your...'

'Shh!' said Thomas, 'Someone will hear you!'

William stopped, then continued in a hushed voice.

'Twelve of the clock
Look well to your locks,
Your fire and your light
And God give you Good Night!'

He gave a little bow and grinned. 'See, I could do it! Only you would know I'm a ghost!'

'How could we arrange it?' Thomas was warming to the idea.

'Simple! Just a phone call from whoever fixes these things to say they've found someone after all.'

'How could we get them to do that?' asked Thomas.

'We wouldn't; don't you see? *I* would make the call!'

'Cool!' said Thomas getting excited, 'When will you do it?'

'As soon as you find out the telephone number.'

William picked up his new cellphone and gazed at it admiringly.

'Then you can leave the rest to me!' he said with a smile.

'Quiet everyone!' Mrs Ward clapped her hands

and waited for silence. 'This afternoon I have a special treat for you. I've managed to arrange a visitor after all. William the Watchman is coming to tell us about his life in Tudor times!'

Over lunch, the chatter was all about the visitor. Thomas had to pretend to be as surprised as his friends.

At two o'clock, William glided invisibly up to the school gate. He crossed the playground and stood behind the huge trunk of the chestnut tree, then, out of sight of the building, he quickly materialized. It had been easy to conceal his bell and lantern under his tunic, but he'd had to ask Thomas to bring his staff the evening before and hide it somewhere safe.

William found his staff lying in a narrow space between the caretaker's shed and the fence, just as Thomas had told him it would be. He straightened his tunic and tweaked his hat, then picked up the tools of his trade and strode purposefully across the playground to the main door.

'William the Watchman from 'People of Past Times' agency,' he announced to the disembodied voice over the intercom.

Buzz, click - an unseen hand opened the door.

'Spooky!' William chuckled as he stepped

inside.

A woman poked her head through a hatch in the wall. 'Good afternoon,' she said. 'What a marvelous costume! Two children are coming to take you to year five's classroom.'

William smiled politely. Little did she know he hadn't had to dress up at all. Not like the time he went undercover as Miss Tudor...

There came the sound of footsteps hurrying along the corridor. Round the corner appeared

a small girl in red jeans and a blue shirt with
Thomas hurrying behind her. Both stopped at the
sight of William, and Thomas tried not to laugh.

'We'll show you where to go,' said the girl.

'Lead on!' said William grandly, giving Thomas
a mischievous wink.

On the way to the classroom they passed a boy
with a pile of registers, heading for the office.

'Hurry up Danny, William the Watchman's
here!' the girl said to him.

'Coming,' said the boy as he passed.

'My job was to patrol the streets at night,'
William told the class sitting before him in rapt
attention. 'There were hundreds of crimes every
year but there was no police force in those days.
With my faithful dog Patch, I kept watch for
anyone up to no good: cut-purses, vagabonds
and the like. When they were caught, offenders
were sent before a Justice of the Peace, and then
punished.'

He went on to tell them all about how different
life was in Tudor Times from life today. The
children were enthralled; no one but William
noticed Danny slip into the room and take his

place at the back.

'Did you ever see Queen Elizabeth I?' one child asked.

Mrs Ward laughed. 'William wasn't alive then!' she said. 'But he knows so much about the times you could almost believe he was.'

When his talk was over, she thanked him for coming and William said goodbye to the children, feeling very pleased he'd given them a good presentation.

'Thomas, would you like to show our visitor the way out please?' said Mrs Ward.

There was no one in the corridor; all the children were busy in their classrooms.

'That was great!' Thomas said. 'What do you think of my school?'

William peeped in through the classroom windows.

'It's marvelous! Everywhere is so bright,' he said. 'I like all the pictures on the walls.'

They turned a corner and were back at the main entrance.

'Are you absolutely sure?' asked a man's voice.

'Yes, it was right there on my desk. A few minutes after the children collected the visitor, I came through to your office to pick up some letters. When I came back, there was no sign of it!'

Thomas and William could see through the hatch. The man and woman had their backs to them.

'That's Mr Price, the principal,' whispered Thomas.

'I wonder what the problem is?' said William.

Thomas glanced through the hatch to see Mr Price and his secretary on their hands and knees, searching desperately for whatever was missing.

'It looks like they've lost something,' he said.

'I hope they find it,' said William. 'A friend of mine lost his head once. He was very upset.'

Thomas laughed, and reached for the button to open the door.

'No need,' said William as he glided through.

'Bye,' whispered Thomas. 'I'll pop round and see you after school.'

Outside, William looked around. Satisfied no one was watching, he dove behind the shed where he hid his staff, lantern and bell.

'Something's afoot,' he told himself. 'And I need to find out what!' He made himself invisible and glided straight through the closed door back into school.

Suddenly, the school seemed to be in a real

commotion. The children were all being assembled in the hall and a grave Mr Price stood facing them.

'I'm afraid something terrible has happened,' he announced once they were all in place. 'The money we have collected for the new soccer strip is missing!'

There was a loud gasp, as the children looked at each other in disbelief.

'Please be alert. There is a slim chance it has been accidentally mislaid and might turn up. We are looking for a yellow cloth bag full of coins and notes. I was going to take it to the bank on my way home.'

William looked at the sad faces of Thomas and his friends as they listened to the principal's grave news.

'There's no time to lose,' he decided. 'I must get on with my investigations straight away!'

He reached the office just as a police officer arrived to speak to Mr Price.

'I see you have a surveillance camera; if someone came in here we should be able to discover who it was.'

Mr Price shuffled his feet uncomfortably. 'I'm afraid that won't help,' he said. 'Our new caretaker hasn't got to grips with the system yet and this office camera wasn't working at the time.'

'Oh no,' said the officer. 'What about the children and the teachers, did any of them see anything?'

'No. Everyone was in their classrooms when the money disappeared.'

'And the visitor?'

'He was giving his talk when this must have happened,' said Mr Price.

The officer made a few notes on his pad. 'I'll take a look around,' he said, 'but I'm not very

hopeful. This is a real mystery.'

'I remember something else,' said the secretary. 'My pot of pens and pencils had fallen over; they'd scattered everywhere!'

'Interesting,' said William making a mental note. He decided to take a look around the school. He found the caretaker in his room making a cup of tea.

'Off you go now Poppy, it's my break time,' said the man, gently removing a black cat from his chair. The cat arched her back indignantly and stalked off.

'The school cat!' said William to himself. 'I'll bet she sees a great deal of what goes on around here. It's a pity she can't talk!'

He glided into the computer suite where he found Thomas's class busy doing some work for their history project. Standing behind Thomas, William watched him type 'Elizerbethan England.' The ghost's fingers itched; he just could not help himself. He reached over and typed 'Elizabethan.'

'Oh!' Lucky, no one noticed Thomas jump.

'Thomas, it's me, sorry I couldn't resist it,' William whispered.

'Thought you'd gone home,' Thomas typed.

'I know about the money. I'll speak to you later.'

'I'll come to the manor after soccer practice,' was the message on the screen.

'Finish up now,' said Mrs Ward. 'It's almost home time.'

William went outside and collected his lantern and bell. He made sure his staff was well hidden behind the shed. As he crossed the playground, children were spilling out from various parts of the building. A group of boys carrying soccer boots were heading for a small wooden pavilion next to the field.

'It's a rubbish game anyway!' Danny called to them as he headed for the gate.

'Oh dear,' said William. 'I wonder what that's all about. I'll get back to the manor and wait for Thomas; he'll tell me.'

Back in his attic, he took down his notebook, pen and ink pot from the shelf. 'Now let me see what have I learned so far...' He turned to a clean page and dipped his quill into the ink pot. He paused to think, pen poised above the pristine paper.

Plop! Before he had even begun to write, a large blob of ink hit the paper. He moved down a couple of lines, trailing his cuff in the wet ink.

'Oh my,' he said, staring at the messy black smudges. With a sigh, he began to write:

Problem – Money missing from the school

office.

Secretary - out the room for only a short time; pens and pencils scattered about.

Caretaker- new to the job; unsure of surveillance system when money went missing.

Did it happen after or before Danny returned to the classroom? Why was he so rude about soccer to the other boys?

'There's a great deal to think about,' said William as he replaced his notebook on the shelf.

The door opened slowly and Thomas peeped round. He looked worried.

'Did you have a good practice?' asked William.

'It was OK,' said Thomas but we have our first

match next week and we'll have to wear the old strip. You won't guess what happened afterwards. I overheard Mr Price talking to his secretary and I think they suspect YOU!'

William froze.

'ME?' he cried, a hand pressed to his chest. 'But that's preposterous! Why would they suspect me? They know I was in the classroom when the money went missing.'

'Mrs Ward phoned the agency to thank them for your visit and discovered they hadn't sent anyone. Mr Price is not sure how, but he's convinced you must be involved!'

'Well, they won't have any luck searching for me. They're on the wrong track.' He glided up and down the attic. 'I must think... Tell me, why did Danny shout at you all on his way home?'

'He was upset because he wasn't picked for the team this time. He does like soccer really.'

'But that's not the way to behave!' said William. 'He should go along to the practices, then he might be picked the next time...'

'He said he was going to buy a new computer game,' said Thomas.

'Really?' said William, 'That is interesting.'

'You don't think Danny took the money do

you?'

'I do hope not. I'm not sure he had the opportunity anyway, it's all to do with timing!'

'I have to go now,' said Thomas. 'What will you do next?'

'After dark, I'll collect my staff and I may just have another look around. Let's meet up tomorrow after school and see if either of us has come up with new evidence.'

'Right,' said Thomas, 'I'll see you then.'

✻✻✻

At nine o'clock that evening, William glided down onto the playground. There were lights on inside the school building and just one car, parked near the gate.

'The caretaker's working late,' remarked William. 'I'll see what he's doing.'

A shutter covered the hatch, so he had to walk a little way along the corridor to peep through the office windows. Before he came to the first window, he noticed something shiny up on the wall in the corner, where the corridor turned.

'It's a mirror and I can see the doors behind me. If I wasn't invisible, I'd be able to see myself coming along. Goodness, I can see into the office too, and round the corner. Now that's useful; when there are lines of children moving around they can avoid any collisions.' He stopped to watch the reflection of the caretaker as he moved around the office. It wasn't very clear what he was doing so William glided forward and looked in through the window. He was climbing a step ladder to reach the camera.

'Better late than never, I suppose,' William said. The caretaker climbed down and walked over to the computer on the desk. He quickly pressed a few keys on the pad then walked off.

William waited until the caretaker left then went into the office. There was a big desk with a computer, trays of papers and the pot of pens and pencils. At the far end of the desk was a shredding machine and next to it, standing on the floor, was a large bin more than half full of shredded paper.

'Everything looks normal to me.' William glanced up at the camera. 'It's a good job I can make myself invisible,' he said. He felt a bit tired and the padded black leather chair by the desk looked comfortable and inviting. 'Just five minutes,' he said. As he sat down the seat swung round to the left. 'It's like a merry-go-round!' he cried, pushing his foot against the leg of the

desk. He'd once tried a merry-go-round in the
playground at the park.

The chair spun round and William rose higher
until it stopped with a jolt. William stood up. He
suddenly felt embarrassed; it was hardly the way
for a great detective to behave. He glanced up at
the camera again; it hadn't occurred to him until
now that although *he* couldn't be seen, the chair
would appear to be moving all by itself. Too late to
worry about that.

'Oops!' he staggered a little until he found his
balance. 'I'm a bit d-dizzy!' He steadied himself
by the desk until he had regained his composure.

'It was fun though,' he chuckled, 'but I'd better
get back to work...'

He took another careful look around the office, and then went through the adjoining door to Mr Price's room. He crossed the room to the letter tray on the desk then turned to walk back.

'That took less than a minute. Whoever stole the money would have to be quick; that is IF the secretary is telling the truth!' Mmm - he hadn't thought of her as a suspect until now. Back in the corridor he headed for the way out. There was another camera above the door and pointing straight at him; he pulled a face and waved cheekily. As he glided out onto the playground, he heard the church clock strike ten. He collected his staff and walked to the gate.

Pausing, he looked up and down the deserted street. All seemed quiet, but if he did meet anyone on the walk home a staff marching along by itself might frighten them half to death.

'I know, I'll ride home like a witch on a broomstick!' He chuckled as he stood astride his staff and gripped it tight. With one push of his feet, he shot into the air. Above the town he flew along, his staff silhouetted against the moonlit sky. 'I hope no one looks up,' he said.

He swooped down onto the bridge by the manor and made his way quietly up to his attic. There was a light on in the long gallery; Mr Grimshaw was enjoying a game of nine-pins. When all the rumbling and clattering ceased, William took down his writing tools and prepared to update his notes.

'Oh my, I must try to be more careful.' He had closed his notebook before the ink was dry and the page was decorated with what looked like the bodies of several dead spiders. He decided to begin a new page yet again!

Suspects –

Splat! A blob of ink hit the page as he paused to think. 'Oh no!'

He began again on a new line.

Suspects:

Danny – Well he did

have money to buy a computer game.

Secretary - Probably thinks no one would suspect her, but she did have the opportunity.

Caretaker - I wonder; could he be pretending not to know how the cameras work, as a cover to steal the money?

William read through his notes again; there were possible suspects but no real evidence. He looked at the picture of Sherlock vainly hoping for some inspiration.

'Perhaps a mug of warm milk would help me sleep. A detective needs his rest and things may seem clearer in the morning.' Down in the kitchen he waited impatiently for the ping. He'd learned to use the microwave by watching Mrs Krupp in the kitchen. Now he took his comforting drink and sat on his chair, thoughtfully nibbling a cookie in between sips. He yawned, emptied his mug and rested his head against the threadbare old cushion as he drifted off to sleep...

'It's elementary, my dear William!' He woke suddenly to a voice inside his head repeating the sentence over and over. In his dreams he had found himself in a hall of mirrors. As he moved from one to another, his image was distorted in different, amusing ways. Tall, thin, wavy William became short, fat William, and one mirror even turned him upside down. As the images faded the voice woke him.

'Sherlock?' he mumbled, rubbing his eyes as he looked at the picture on the wall. He recalled how Sherlock Holmes used the same expression to Dr Watson when explaining his theories; was Sherlock trying to tell *him* something? He racked his brains trying to recall every tiny detail from the evening before. Suddenly he jumped up from his chair. 'Why'd I not think of that?' he cried.

Down the stairs he glided and out into the courtyard. It was still dark as he sped along the high street. As he passed the church, he was surprised to see the clock said only ten minutes past five. On he went until he reached the school where one security light still shone in the reception area. Once inside, William materialized and looked up at the mirror in the corner where the corridor turned. He could see his reflection and, as he had hoped, the reflection of the camera above the front door behind him. But where did the pictures go to? He scratched his head and thought about it. He remembered how the caretaker had done something on the computer after fiddling with the camera in the office.

'I wonder...' William glided off to the office. He stood before the desk and looked at the monitor. What a surprise! He could see himself in the room. He stretched out his hand and touched the keyboard.

'OH!' he cried, jumping back as the picture changed to the view from the camera above the front door. He could see the corridor now and the mirror where the corridor turned a corner.

'This is all very well,' he said out loud, 'but how do I look at pictures from days before?'

He could see words along the top of the screen. One said 'help' but it wasn't any help at all if he didn't know how to point to the word. He sat down on the chair and looked around the desk. There

was a black oval thing that glowed red and seemed
to be attached to the computer with a wire. He
remembered Thomas using one in the computer
suite, but what did it do?

'I know, I'll phone him and ask.'

Thomas jumped awake at the sound of his
cellphone. *Meow! Meow! Meow!*

'Hello...' he said sleepily.

'Thomas, what's this black thing with a red light
next to the computer keyboard?'

'What's going on? Where are you?' Thomas
rubbed his eyes and looked at his alarm clock. 'It's
half past five in the morning!'

William explained.

'Oh, I see. The black thing is a mouse.'

'A MOUSE?'

'Not the kind of mouse you think,' yawned Thomas. Blinking to clear the sleep from his eyes, he explained to William how to use the mouse.

William moved it carefully and a little arrow appeared on the screen and moved about. He soon found he could control the arrow by moving the mouse. He pointed at 'help' and pressed. Words appeared on the screen, but he couldn't make any sense of them. He tried 'file' instead. Now this looked more hopeful. There was a list of dates. He found the date for the day when the money was stolen and pointed the arrow at it. *Click.*

'Right, Thomas, I think I have what I want. Thanks for your help.' He switched off his cellphone.

Moving closer to the screen, he looked at the picture that appeared. Yes, he could see the mirror and whatever was reflected in it but not very clear. He saw the backs of himself and the children on the way to class. Then he saw Danny approaching with the pile of registers. He did not enter the office. He just placed the registers on a table by the door and set off back.

William peered into the depths of the picture. Danny walked past the mirror, round the corner

and along the other corridor. William could just
see the inside of the office in the mirror. Nothing
moved at first, but then suddenly something black
skidded across the desk and vanished. William
watched the recording over again. 'Well how about
that!' he cried with glee.

In the secretary's office he stood puzzling as
he gazed at the desk. He knew now Poppy the cat
was responsible for scattering the pens and pencils
everywhere. 'So she could easily have knocked
the bag of money off the desk,' he said to himself.
'But where did it go?'

He remembered there had been no sign of it on
the floor. He circled the desk looking for clues. 'Of
course - the shredder bin! I wonder....' He delved
deep in among the shreds of paper. 'Eureka!' he
shouted, holding the yellow bag aloft. 'I have it!'

William replaced the bag under the shredded
paper in the bin, leaving plenty of paper spilling
over the sides. Then he sat invisible in the corner
of the office and waited until the secretary arrived
in the morning.

Just as he had hoped, she called for the
caretaker as soon she saw the overflowing bin.

'It's like a paper storm in here!' she said.

The caretaker grasped the top of the black garbage bag and began to lift it from the bin. William saw his chance. Diving forward, he knocked the bin from the caretaker's hand. The sack tipped up and the paper spilled out everywhere.

'Hey! W-what's going on..?'

'You clumsy man,' shouted the secretary. 'It will all have to be picked up! ...Oh look!' She was pointing at the yellow bag lying in a nest of paper on the floor. 'Goodness!'

'So you see,' said William, munching on a cookie, 'it was all done by mirrors!'

'Mr Price told us they'd found the money in the trash,' said Thomas, 'but they have no idea how it got there.'

127

'They'll probably never find out,' said William, 'it's our secret!'

'Clever deduction, William!'

'Elementary, my dear Thomas! But I couldn't have managed without your help. It's a good job we have our cellphones.'

'We will have the new strip in time for the match next week. Will you come to watch?'

'Of course,' said William.

'And it's good news about Danny. He's promised to come to the practices. He knows he can't be picked every time!'

'So all turned out well in the end,' said William with a smile, as he reached for another cookie.

The Baker's Boy Affair

William looked out through the attic window. Who would have believed such a beautiful, calm morning could follow such a wild, windy night? Fall leaves were scattered everywhere like a giant golden carpet. The huge oak tree in front of the church was stripped almost bare, so he could just make out the time on the tower clock.

'Half past seven, and here comes Sam!'

A boy aged about sixteen came riding a bicycle over the bridge. His feet left the pedals as he flew down the slope and round the corner out of sight. William heard the scrunch of gravel as the bicycle came to a halt.

'Time for breakfast and it couldn't be fresher!' His stomach rumbled in anticipation. He arrived in the café just in time to see Sam enter with a huge

tray of warm croissants.

'Mrs Brown said to tell you they only came
out the oven at quarter past,' he announced to
Mrs Krupp as he placed the tray on the table. Mrs
Krupp smiled and handed him one of the delicious
treats as a reward.

'I can always rely on you Sam,' she said. 'Hurry
along now or you will miss the school bus.'

William knew all about Sam from Thomas. He
lived at Home Farm next to the manor and earned
pocket money delivering bread around the village.
He attended Lockley High School. On Saturdays
he worked at the bakery all morning. On school

days, he did an early delivery to the manor and after school would spend an hour helping Mrs Brown tidy the shop and prepare for the next day.

As soon as Mrs Krupp's back was turned, William helped himself to a croissant. As he tucked it under his tunic, she began to unload the tray.

'Twenty-two....that's strange; our order is for two dozen. There should be twenty-three left.' She looked around the deserted café, her eyes narrowing.

'It's you again, isn't it! Leave my croissants alone!' William ducked away and headed back to the attic.

'Well, Sherlock,' he said to the picture of the great detective, 'things are a bit quiet right now. I could do with another case to solve...'

After school, Thomas arrived, breathless from running. 'Sam is in trouble!' he gasped.

'Oh my, what happened?' asked William.

'This morning, when they were getting onto the bus there was a great deal of jostling and everyone was talking at once. Someone shouted to the driver that Sam would not be coming, so he drove off without him. When Sam eventually arrived at school he was told to stay behind tonight to catch up with his work, so he won't be able to do his job at the bakery this evening!'

'Poor Sam, and it wasn't his fault! Do you know who shouted?'

'No, but they must have known it would cause trouble.'

'How unkind!' William said. 'Let me know if you hear of more problems. Have you any other news?'

'Well, there's a new girl called Rosie in my class. She has a brother called Jason at the High School. They've come to live in one of the houses at the end of the village. Oh, and we started a new bit of our topic today; I don't suppose you can tell me anything about Sir Walter Raleigh?' Thomas grinned and took out his homework book.

'You know very well I can!' laughed William.

'Saturday!' said William jumping up from his chair. 'I love Saturdays.' He rushed to the window and looked out. 'I'd better hurry, it's nearly time for kick off!' He was gliding past the ticket office heading for the front door when he stopped suddenly.

'Sam, oh yes, he's been here. He delivered the café order ages ago. Sorry I can't help.' Mavis put the phone down and went back to her typing.

'I wonder what that was about,' thought William.

As he glided down the lane toward the village he caught up with someone pushing a bicycle; it was Sam. Why wasn't he riding? William could see the front tire was absolutely flat.

'Oh my, I wish I could help. There are orders in his basket still to be delivered.' He didn't like to leave the boy so walked alongside him until they reached the garage.

'Well it's not a puncture,' said Mr Smith, the owner, scratching his head. 'If you ask me,

someone has let your tire down!' He pumped some air into the tire; Sam thanked him and quickly pedaled off on his rounds. William watched as a white van came tearing up the road. It flew past the garage and overtook Sam at such a speed the bike wobbled precariously.

'Mad man!' shouted Mr Smith.

'Road hog!' joined in William, standing just

behind him. The garage owner swung round in surprise but there was no one to be seen.

'Who was that?' He shivered as a sudden cool breeze whipped up the leaves on the ground and sent them chasing round and round his feet. 'Spooky,' he said. 'I think I could do with a strong cup of tea.'

William arrived at the field just as the whistle blew for half time. Thomas walked toward him sucking a piece of orange. He knew exactly where his invisible friend would be standing.

'What's the score?' asked William. 'I'm afraid I've only just arrived.' He went on to explain about Sam.

'You haven't missed much,' said Thomas. 'It's nil/nil. Coach says we'd better liven up in the second half!' He was quiet for a short time. 'William, do you think someone is trying to cause trouble for Sam?'

'Well,' said William, 'I've been thinking about that. Two incidents in one week make me suspicious. I'm going to keep a special eye on him.'

The whistle blew and Thomas ran off to join his team. The second half was much better. Both teams played well, so the two all draw was a fair result. William joined in the cheering then glided off to the bakery to find out how Sam was getting on. There was no sign of his bike outside. 'He must still be out on his rounds,' thought William.

He glided into the shop and past the line of customers waiting to be served by the young assistant. Mrs Brown was speaking on the telephone in the little office next to the bakery.

'I'm sorry your bloomers are missing, Miss

Prim. I'm sure they were in the tray when Sam set off. As soon as he arrives back I will send more.'

'Bloomers?' said William. 'In a bakery? What will they be selling next?' He followed Mrs Brown into the shop and watched her take two oval shaped loaves from the shelf. He read the sign above them: BLOOMERS - 98p.

'Oh, I see,' he laughed. 'That's a funny name for a loaf of bread.' He was still chuckling as he left the shop. Sam was just cycling into the entry that led to the yard at the back of the shop so William followed.

'Sam,' said Mrs Brown, 'where have you been all this time and what happened to Miss Prim's bloomers?'

'Sorry,' said Sam. 'Someone let my tire down. I don't know what happened to Miss Prim's bread. I took the cakes in first. When I went back for the loaves there was no sign of them. I think Miss Prim thought I'd dropped them somewhere but I'm sure I didn't.'

'Oh my, well whatever happened, you will have to take ...' The phone rang. 'Hello, Brown's Bakery, may I help you?' There was a pause while the person on the other end spoke. 'Very well, Miss Prim, I understand. Goodbye.'

Mrs Brown turned to Sam with a sorrowful face.

'It seems a man in a white van just called on Miss Prim. He was selling bread and cakes from a new shop somewhere in Lockley, so she bought bloomers from him! Dear me, what is going on?' Poor Sam did not know what to say; he set off for home feeling very dejected.

✱✱✱

After enjoying his own lunch of a bacon roll from the café, William took down his quill and ink pot from the shelf and opened his notebook.

'New case, new page,' he said, carefully wiping off the surplus ink from the nib, and began on the very top line.

The Case of the Missing Bloomers, he wrote in the style of his hero. It sounded mysterious enough but it wasn't just about the bloomers was it? He crossed it out and began a new line.

The Case of... What was it the case of? It all seemed a bit confusing. He would write down the facts and think what to call it later.

Problems:
1. Someone made Sam miss the school bus and he couldn't do his job at the bakery - was it just a prank?
2. Someone let the air out Sam's tire and made him late on his rounds.
3. Someone took Miss Prim's bloomers.
4. Someone in a white van is trying to take Mrs Brown's customers. A white van almost knocked Sam off his bike.

William stopped writing to think for a short time, his pen poised ready for the next word.

Plop! A blob of ink hit the page.

'Oops! I must be more careful.' He missed several lines to avoid the splashes then continued to write.

Facts:
1. The only people on the bus besides the driver were school children so one of them must have shouted.
2. It was a white van that nearly knocked Sam off his bike. It was a white van that called at Miss Prim's house.

Suspects:
1. No clues as to which child shouted on the bus.
2. Could it be the same white van in both incidents? If so, the driver

could be trying to prevent Sam from doing his job properly so he can steal the customers.

William replaced his quill pen in the ink pot and read his notes over and over. 'This is all very puzzling,' he told Sherlock. 'I think I'll go stroll in the park to clear my head; Thomas might be there.'

Some children, who looked a little younger than Thomas, were playing on the swings. William saw one of the Lockely High School boys approaching.

'I think it's my turn now,' he said to a little girl. He grabbed one of the chains holding the seat and stopped her swinging. The girl slid from the seat and ran off, crying. He sat on the swing and glared at the other children who quickly retreated to a corner of the playground.

'Leave them alone, Jason!' shouted a voice. William looked round to see Sam approaching.

'And what are you going to do about it?' The boy glared at Sam defiantly and idly pushed at the ground with one foot as he swung slowly backwards and forwards. Before Sam could reply, the swing gave a sudden jerk and shot forward, high in the air. 'Hey, what's happening?' Jason hung on as the swing rose higher and higher. Suddenly it seemed to stop dead at the highest point and he left the seat and took off like a rocket. 'Ahh!' he shouted as he soared through the air and landed head first in the sand pit.

There was silence for a short time as he struggled to his feet then everyone watching burst out laughing. Pale faced, Jason staggered toward Sam. 'You won't be laughing when I've finished with you,' he muttered as he walked off.

'What was all that about, Sam?' It was Thomas.

'That new boy, Jason, is a bully. He took a swing from a little girl.'

'What did you do?'

'I told him to leave the children alone but he wasn't taking any notice. Then something a bit spooky happened; he seemed to lose control of the swing and ended up in the sand pit! I think he was real scared, but he tried not to show it.'

'Serves him right,' said Thomas, who knew at once who was responsible for the punishment. He went to sit on a seat in a quiet corner of the playground.

'Hello,' said a voice.

'William, I guessed it must be you doing spooky things!'

'I don't think he'll go on the swings again for a while,' laughed William. 'But he did threaten Sam afterward; I'm worried about that.'

'His sister told me he was in trouble at school for taking snacks from children in her class at playtime on Friday,' said Thomas.

'Mmm,' said William. 'He seems to enjoy upsetting people. Do you know if he was on the bus the day Sam missed it?'

'I think he was. Do you think it could have been him who shouted to the driver?'

'Sounds like his kind of trick,' William said. 'See if you can find out more about this Jason.'

***

On Thursday morning William woke early as he had done every day that week. He was already sitting in the café when Sam arrived with the croissants. He swiftly took one off to his room but didn't stop to eat it.

'Breakfast will have to wait,' he said. 'I'm going to follow Sam again to see him safe on the bus.' He'd done that each day since Monday and so far the week had been uneventful. He hurried back downstairs and caught up with the bakery bicycle on the bridge. When they reached Home Farm, Sam would stop to pick up his school bag on his way back to the village then he would leave the bike in the bakery yard before catching the school bus. This morning, things did not go according to plan. As they rounded the bend before the farm gate Sam slammed on his brakes to avoid ploughing into some sheep wandering all over the road.

'Goodness,' said William, 'that was nearly a nasty accident. I wonder how they've escaped.' The gate to the field was closed. Sam opened it and started to round up the sheep but it was not easy; no matter how he tried, there was always one ran the wrong way.

'Oh no!' he shouted in desperation. 'Silly sheep! I'm going to be late!'

William joined in; when Sam was not looking, he glided alongside one of the wayward sheep and guided it through the gate. If it hadn't been for William's help the job would have taken twice as long. When Sam ran inside to get his bag, William saw a boy appear from behind a bush and run off toward the village; it was Jason. He chased him up the lane toward main street.

'That's odd,' he said. 'This is not Jason's usual way to the bus stop. He lives in one of the new

houses at the other end of the village; could he have let the sheep out to make Sam miss his bus?'

The bus came round the corner toward them and stopped to pick up the line of children. Jason quickened his pace; he had almost reached the crossing. All he had to do was cross the road and join the tail end of the line. William glanced over his shoulder; Sam was still a speck in the distance.

The crossing guard saw Jason approaching and turned to pick up his sign ready to stop the traffic but it was no longer propped against the wall; the sign had vanished. Jason stood helpless as the stream of cars taking people to work drove past without a break. Sam came cycling up and turned right before the crossing. Luckily, the bus had held up the traffic on that side of the road and he was able to turn easily. The bakery was just round the corner. He left the bike in the yard and ran as fast as he could.

He came round the corner just as the bus was about to pull out but the driver saw him and waited. Sam leapt aboard and the bus moved off. On the other side of the road, Jason watched helpless. The crossing guard retrieved his sign from over the wall where it had somehow ended up half hidden in long grass, but it was too late; the bus had gone.

'I wonder who'll be staying at school to catch up with work tonight,' chuckled William as he made his way back to the manor for breakfast.

But Jason didn't even bother to go to school. Later that morning, William saw him in the park talking to someone on his cell phone. He finished the conversation and set off at a jog to the far gate that opened onto Keepers Lane. William followed.

A white van was waiting at the gate and Jason climbed into the passenger seat. The van did not move. After a few minutes Jason emerged with a carrier bag and set off on foot. He waved to the driver as the van took the Lockley road.

'I wonder what you are up to now,' said William. 'I'll not let you out my sight until I find out!' His stomach reminded him it was already past lunchtime; thank goodness he had had the foresight to put a few cookies in his pocket.

Jason took a piece of paper from the bag and put it in Patrick's mailbox. He carried on from house to house until his bag was almost empty then he sat down on the shoulder of the road and took a bar of candy from his pocket. He didn't notice one of the leaflets float out his bag and disappear.

'*Dough To Door!*' read the leaflet. '*Get your*

bread delivered daily!'

As soon as William read it, he went straight along to the bakery to see what was happening there.

He found Mrs Brown on her hands and knees rummaging in the waste paper bin. When Sam arrived she asked, 'Have you seen the list of customer orders for Saturday? I'm sure it was pinned on the board this morning, but I can't find it anywhere!'

'It was there this morning, before I went to the manor,' said Sam. 'I saw it.' He helped Mrs Brown search but the paper could not be found.

'Oh my, I'll have to phone as many people as I can think of tomorrow and try to sort it out.' She gave up the search and she and Sam did their usual jobs to make the shop ready for the next day.

'Oh, Sherlock!' William told his hero when he got back to the attic. 'There's major trouble brewing. I must go to the bakery tomorrow and see what develops...'

Woof! Woof! Woof!

William swung round. A dog in his attic?

Woof! Woof!

'Oh, it's my cellphone,' he laughed. 'Hello Thomas.'

'William. I can't come round because I've too much homework, but I've something to report!'

'Go ahead, Watson!'

Thomas grinned to himself. He was pleased when William called him Watson after the great Sherlock's assistant. 'This morning, on my way to school, I was surprised to see Jason coming from the entry leading to the bakery yard. The bus to Lockley High School had already left.'

'Ah yes,' interrupted William. 'He did miss the bus!' he chuckled.

'Oh,' laughed Thomas, 'and I'll bet you had something to do with that!'

'I may have...' said William. He went on to tell Thomas about the sheep.

'There's something else,' said Thomas. 'I saw Jason stuff a piece of paper in his pocket. It looked rather suspicious.'

'Mmm,' said William. 'So he was coming from the direction of the bakery and he had a piece of paper. Do you know, I think I know what that paper was! Well done, Watson!'

'What will you do next?' Thomas asked.

'Wait and see,' William said. He felt sure he

would know what to do when the time came. 'Bye for now, see you soon!'

'Bye,' said Thomas.

William took down his quill pen and notebook.

'Now let me see, there are new developments to report...'

Facts:

1. Sam almost missed the bus because someone let the sheep out.

2. Jason was near the farm. Later, he met the van driver and mailed the leaflets advertising special offers.

3. Mrs Brown's list of orders went missing.

4. Thomas saw Jason coming from the baker's yard with a piece of paper.

'Now what can I deduce from all this?' he

asked himself, reaching for another cookie. After popping it into his mouth, he continued to write...

> 1. Jason could have let the sheep out.
> 2. He is working for the driver of a white van who appears to be stealing Mrs Brown's customers!
> 3. Did Jason take Mrs Brown's customer list while she was busy opening the shop?
> Action:
> Go to the bakery tomorrow and see what's happening. Watch out for Jason and the white van man.

William replaced his notebook and pen on the shelf.

'Now for an early night I think. I'm going to need my wits about me to solve this puzzle!'

***

On Friday morning, Sam turned up to find Mrs Brown sitting in the office looking very worried.

'I'm afraid there's no work for you this Saturday, Sam. Before I had a chance to phone my customers they phoned me to cancel their orders.'

'But why?' asked Sam.

'It seems they've had a better offer,' she said bitterly.

William sat quietly in the corner, listening. Tonight he would make a plan and tomorrow he would put his plan into action. He wasn't beaten yet!

***

On Saturday morning William saw a white van drive over the bridge. He glided down to the café in time to see a man place a tray of croissants on the table in the kitchen.

'Bread delivery!' he shouted. A voice from the café called a thank you.

William could see Mrs Krupp wiping tables. The van driver left the kitchen by the back door.

'Not a second to lose!' said William. He flew out and grabbed a tray of Cornish pasties from the back of the van just as the driver drove off. He swapped them with the tray in the kitchen and, with the croissants under his cloak, flew off at high speed to catch the truck.

The next delivery was to the Great Hardleigh Hotel. The driver delivered Danish pastries for the guests' breakfasts. Quick as a flash, when no one was looking, William substituted the pastries for croissants; the guests would not be getting their favorites today. Next, the van pulled up outside the Farmers Arms where the driver delivered a tray of meat pies.

'They look good,' said Mr Fletcher. 'I have plenty of orders for meat pies on Saturday lunchtime.' But as he went off to do his jobs around the bar, the meat pies were quickly swapped for iced buns.

Miss Prim's vegetarian roll became a meat pie and Thomas's gran complained all she had for Joe's packed lunch was a vegetarian slice instead of the delicious cornish pasty he'd been expecting. That was the first Thomas knew of any problems that morning. He figured he'd better phone William and tell him.

'Don't worry,' said William. 'It's all part of the

plan! I can't stop now. There's too much going on. Meet me in the attic in an hour.'

By the time the white van man had finished his rounds the telephone in Mrs Brown's office wouldn't stop ringing. One after another of her customers apologized for deserting her and asked if she could help them sort out their problems.

'I'd better phone for Sam,' she said. 'I could do with his help!' Sam came straight away and was soon busy on his rounds putting things right.

William returned to his attic for a well deserved break. When Thomas arrived he was carrying a large paper bag.

'Cakes,' he said. 'When I passed the bakery Mrs Brown had a special offer - buy one get one free! She said it is to celebrate having her customers back. I'm not sure what happened, William, you'll have to explain.'

'Jason played hookey on Thursday. After you saw him near the bakery, he delivered some leaflets for the man in the white truck. He had stolen the list of orders from the bakery office – that was the piece of paper you saw him stuff into his pocket. When I saw what was written on the leaflets, I knew Brown's Bakery would suffer.

The special offers were too much to resist for Mrs Brown's customers and they cancelled their orders with her.'

'So how did she get her customers back?' Thomas asked.

William described the morning's events.

'So it was all up to you, just as I suspected! Where's Jason now?'

'I don't know,' said William, 'probably keeping out the way for a while. He's in enough trouble for playing hookey, and if anyone finds out he delivered the leaflets...Well let's just say he'd be wise to behave himself from now on. Now what were you saying about cakes?'

✳✳✳

There were just a few days to go before the end of term.

'Mom and Dad are coming to collect me on Saturday,' said Thomas. 'I'll be living back with them from now on.'

'I'll miss you,' said William.

'Don't worry, I'll see you every vacation and in the meantime I have a present for you. I saw it at the second hand book shop.'

'The Clocks – A Hercule Poirot Investigation by Agatha Christie,' read William.

'Poirot was a great detective.'

'And Sherlock,' said William glancing at the great man's picture.

'And you!' said Thomas. 'You're the greatest!'

Watch out for more

Watchman
William
Ghost
Detective

COMING SOON!